W. McDonald

History of Methodism in Providence

Rhode Island, from its introducion in 1787 to 1867

W. McDonald

History of Methodism in Providence
Rhode Island, from its introducion in 1787 to 1867

ISBN/EAN: 9783337378592

Printed in Europe, USA, Canada, Australia, Japan

Cover: Foto ©Andreas Hilbeck / pixelio.de

More available books at **www.hansebooks.com**

OF

METHODISM

IN

PROVIDENCE, RHODE ISLAND,

FROM ITS INTRODUCTION IN

1787 TO 1867.

BY W. McDONALD.

BOSTON:
PHIPPS & PRIDE, PRINTERS.
No. 11 CORNHILL,
1868.

INTRODUCTION.

THE introduction of Methodism into New England was an epoch in its religious history, the results of which we are unable, at present, fully to estimate. The facts and incidents of its early history are deeply interesting, but exceedingly fragmentary, requiring no little amount of labor to collect and arrange in chronological order.

The preparation of this work was commenced at the request of the "Providence District Preacher's Meeting," while the writer was pastor of Chestnut Street Church, and was intended, originally, to be confined to that church. But it was thought best, subsequently, to extend the work and include a brief history of the other Methodist churches in the city. We have done this as best we could, with the materials at our command.

We have encountered, in the preparation of this little volume, great difficulties in fixing the dates of events in the early history of Methodism in this city. We may not have succeeded in every case; but if there has been any mistake, it has resulted from the impossibility of securing the desired information. Our materials have been collected from a great variety of published and unpublished documents, as well as from the lips and pens of many still living. We are under many obligations to Rev. S. Reed, Rev. J. Livesey, Rev. J. D. Butler, Rev. R. W. Allen, Rev. D. H. Ela, Rev. V. A. Cooper, Mrs. Rev. S. Heath, Rev. S. W. Coggeshall, D.D., Hon. Elisha Dyer, Daniel Field, Esq., (late deceased) and others, for valuable information. We have made the best use we were able of the materials at our disposal, and hope the result may not be entirely unsatisfactory to the reader.

W. McDONALD.

Boston, 1868.

HISTORY

CHESTNUT STREET CHURCH.

REV. FREEBORN GARRETTSON.

THE first Methodist preacher to visit and preach in
Providence, was Rev. Freeborn Garrettson, a native
of Maryland; born August 15, 1752. He was edu-
cated in the faith of the Church of England, but
under the searching preaching of Rev. Mr. Straw-
bridge, a Local Methodist preacher from Ireland, he
was deeply awakened, and in June, 1775, was born
again. "The blessed change," he says, "I shall
never forget."

GARRETTSON FREES HIS SLAVES.

By the death of his father he became, without his
consent, a slaveholder. For a time his mind was,
from some cause to him unknown, deeply dejected.
He sought relief in prayer. One evening, about
eight o'clock, he called the family together for prayer.
"As I stood," he says, "with a book in my hand, in

the act of giving out a hymn, this thought powerfully struck my mind : 'It is not right to keep your fellow creatures in bondage ; you must let the oppressed go free.' I knew it to be that same blessed voice which had spoken to me before. Till then I had never suspected that the practice of slave keeping was wrong ; I had not read a book on the subject, nor been told so by any. I paused a minute and then replied, 'Lord, the oppressed shall go free.' And I was as clear of them in my mind as if I had never owned one. I told them they did not belong to me, and that I did not desire their services without compensation. I was now at liberty to proceed in worship. After singing I kneeled to pray. Had I the tongue of an angel, I could not fully describe what I felt. All my dejection, and melancholy gloom which preyed upon me vanished in a moment, and a Divine sweetness ran through my whole frame."

COMMENCES HIS ITINERANT LABOR.

Mr. Garrettson commenced his itinerant labors the same year of his conversion, and for nine years traveled extensively through Maryland, Virginia, North and South Carolina, Pennsylvania, Delaware and New Jersey. He preached with remarkable power, which drew upon him a storm of persecution. Few men suffered more than he. In a letter addressed to Mr. Wesley, he says, "My lot has mostly been cast in new places, to form circuits, which much exposed me to persecution. Once I was imprisoned; twice beaten, left on the highway speechless and senseless; (I must have gone into a world of spirits, had not God in mercy sent a good Samaritan, that bled and took me to a friend's house); once shot at; guns and pistols presented at my breast; once delivered from an armed mob, in the dead time of night, on the highway, by a surprising flash of lightning; surrounded frequently by mobs; stoned frequently; I have had to escape for my life at dead time of night. O! shall I ever forget the divine hand which has supported me?"

GARRETTSON IN NOVA SCOTIA.

At the "Christmas Conference," 1784, Mr. Garrettson, through the influence of Dr. Coke, consented to make a missionary tour into Nova Scotia, and gather into the fold, if possible, the shepherdless sheep whom war had driven into those parts. About the middle of February, in company with James O. Cromwell, he embarked for Halifax, and after a stormy and dangerous passage of thirteen days, they

reached their destination, and commenced their labors.
Mr. Garrettson remained in Nova Scotia about three
years, adding to the society, during the time, about
six hundred members. Of his labors and sufferings
he says, "I traversed the mountains and valleys, frequently on foot, with my knapsack on my back,
guided by Indian paths in the wilderness, when it
was not expedient to take a horse; and I had often
to wade through morasses half leg deep in mud and
water, frequently satisfying my hunger with a piece
of bread and pork from my knapsack, quenching my
thirst from a brook, and resting my weary limbs on
the leaves of the trees. Thanks be to God! he com-
pensated me for all my trial, for many precious souls
were awakened and converted to God."

GARRETTSON IN BOSTON.

April 10th, 1787, Mr. Garrettson sailed for Boston, at which place he arrived, after a perilous passage of three days. He was kindly received by a
few pious friends, and preached a few sermons in
private houses, not being admitted to any of the pul-
pits of the city.

GARRETTSON'S FIRST VISIT TO PROVIDENCE.

April 17th, he left Boston for the South. On his
way, he stopped at Providence, where he says, he

found several who loved the Lord Jesus. He was invited by Rev. Mr. Snow, pastor of the Congregational Church,—who he says, was "a worthy and pious man,"—to preach in his church, which he did twice to a numerous and attentive audience. These it is believed, were the first Methodist sermons ever preached in this city.

Mr. Garrettson stopped on his way at Newport and preached, by invitation, in the meeting house, morning and evening, to a numerous assembly, among whom he rejoiced to find some, as he believed, eminently pious. He then sailed for New York.

JESSE LEE IN RHODE ISLAND.

August 31st, 1789, Jesse Lee says, "I set out on a tour for Rhode Island State, and it was my fervent prayer to God, that if my undertaking was not according to His will, that the houses of the people might be shut against me; but if my journey was right, that God would open the houses and hearts of the people to receive me at my coming." On the 3d day of September he entered Rhode Island, and stopped at Mr. Stanton's, who kept a coffee house in Charleston, Washington County. Here he preached to a congregation of Seventh Day Baptists, from Rev. 3: 20—"Behold I stand at the door and knock." He remained in the State but four days, and remarked on leaving, "I am the first preacher of our way that has ever visited this part of the country." This, doubtless, was true of that part of Rhode Island through which he travelled, but it could not have been true of Providence, as Mr. Garrettson had preached here nearly two years before. In fact, it is quite certain that Mr. Lee did not preach in Providence on his first visit to Rhode Island.

JESSE LEE'S FIRST VISIT TO PROVIDENCE.

In the month of June, 1790, Mr. Lee made a second tour through New England. He entered Rhode Island about the first of July, and preached in Newport, Bristol and Warren, and on the 4th of July preached his first sermon in Providence. For some reason he did not preach in Mr. Snow's meeting house, but preached five times in some private house and several times in the Court House.

LEE, GARRETTSON AND BLACK HARRY MEET.

On the 7th, he left the city for Boston, praying that if his journey to the East was of God, that the houses and hearts of the people might be opened to receive him. When about ten miles from town, he met, unexpectedly, his friend and former fellow la-

borer, Freeborn Garrettson, and his traveling companion, well known in those days as "Black Harry."
Though unexpected, it was a happy meeting.

"I had rode but about thirty miles," says Mr.
Garrettson, "when I met brother Lee, and while
we were sitting on our horses talking, an old gentleman rode up and asked us to go to his house and
preach that night; we went, and had a comfortable
meeting, and I also preached the next morning.
After dinner we parted; brother Lee consented to
go to Boston and make a trial there until I could
send another preacher.

GARRETTSON AND BLACK HARRY IN PROVIDENCE.

"I reached Providence," says Mr. Garrettson,
about five o'clock. The bell rang and I had an opportunity of preaching in good old Mr. Snow's
meeting house."

The next day he had a sweet time in retirement,
and in the evening addressed a larger congregation
than he had addressed the night before. Sunday
the 11th, he preached with freedom in the morning
at 6 o'clock. "I officiated," he says, "all day for
good Mr. Snow, and at six, Harry preached in the
meeting house to more than one thousand people."
Mr. Garrettson preached on the following morning

at 5 o'clock, to about three hundred persons. This was his last sermon in Providence for more than thirty years. He says, "I had a sweet time in Providence. I had no doubt but the Lord began a good work in many hearts. I left many in tears."

"Black Harry," as he is called, who visited Providence with Mr. Garrettson, and preached in Mr. Snow's meeting house, was so remarkable a character as to deserve a brief notice in this place. His proper name was Harry Hosier. He travelled extensively with Asbury, Coke, Whatcoat and Garrettson. He acted as their servant, or driver, and is said to have excelled them all in popularity as a preacher. Dr. Rush, of Philadelphia, pronounced him "the greatest orator in America." He is described as "small in stature, and perfectly black, with eyes of remarkable brilliancy and keenness, and singular readiness and aptness of speech, though unable to read." It frequently occurred that the multitude preferred Black Harry to Asbury himself, Dr. Coke says of him, "I really believe he is one of the best preachers in the world,—there is such an amazing power attends his word, though he cannot read, and he is one of the humblest creatures I ever saw." Mr. Garrettson says of him, "I found the people very curious to hear Harry. I therefore declined preaching, in order that their curiosity might be satisfied." The Quakers thought, as he was unlearned, he must have preached by immediate inspiration. Through the indulgent hospitalities which were lavished upon him, he became temporarily the victim of wine, and fell. But by repentance, and faith in a forgiving God, he recovered himself, and was restored to the Divine favor. He at once resumed his labors and remained faithful unto death, which occurred in the city of Philadelphia about the year 1810. "He was borne to the grave by a great procession of both white and black admirers, who buried him as a hero, once overcome but finally victorious."

ASBURY VISITS PROVIDENCE.

The year 1791 is memorable in our history in Rhode Island as being the year of the first visit of the venerable Asbury to this State. He entered Providence Sunday, June 19, and in the A. M. attended the ministry of Rev. Mr. M———, a Baptist, and in the P. M. that of Rev. Mr. S———, whom he styles a "New Light." The Baptist minister whom he heard in the forenoon, was Rev. Jonathan Maxcy, the youthful pastor of the 1st Baptist Church,

2

and successor of Dr. Manning, the first President of Brown University. Dr. Manning resigned his charge about this time, and Mr. Maxcy, a tutor in Brown, and a youth of twenty-three years, was chosen pastor of the church ; and subsequently, on the death of Dr. Manning, which occurred on the 29th of the following month, was elected President of Brown University.

The "New light," whom he heard in the P. M., was Rev. Mr. Snow, of the Congregational Church. He was a man of a most excellent spirit, and highly esteemed by the early Methodist preachers. He was a Whitefield Congregationalist ; had been converted under the ministry of that holy man—Rev. Gilbert Tennant ;—was a man of deep piety and apostolic zeal. The Methodist ministers were always cordially received by him, and often permitted to preach in his pulpit. In the evening Mr. Asbury preached from Isa. 61 : 1–3 ; "The spirit of the Lord God is upon me," &c. The place of preaching is not mentioned. "I found," he says, "a few gracious souls, and some seeking. It has been a season of deep exercise with me while here. I have had some weighty sensations. I think the Lord will revive his work in Providence." Monday forenoon he visited some serious families.

"The afternoon," he says, "1 spent very agreeably with the old prophet, Mr. Snow, aged about seventy years. He was awakened through the instrumentality of Gilbert Tennant, whose memory I revere. He told me much about Mr. Whitefield, and old times, and of the ministers of old times;—of himself, his awakening and conversion to God; — of his riding thirty miles to Newport, in exceeding cold weather, to bring Mr. Tennant to Providence."

"Having obtained more knowledge of the people," he says, "my subject was Gal. 6 : 14; "But God forbid that I should glory," &c. The sermon was "plain and pointed, and the audience was serious and attentive." The following is the plan of his sermon :

"I endeavored to show :

1. What it is for a man to glory in a thing.
2. What men glory in, which is not the cross of Christ.
3. What it is to glory in the cross of Christ.
4. How a person may know when he glories in the cross of Christ, viz : by the world being crucified to him, and he unto the world."

He continues : "The people here appear to be prudent, active, frugal; cultivating a spirit of good family economy; and they are kind to strangers. They

have had frequent revivals of religion. I had faith
to believe the Lord would shortly visit them again,
and that even we shall have something to do in this
town."

THE FIRST CIRCUIT PREACHER.

In 1792 Providence appears on the "Minutes" for
the first time, with Lemuel Smith preacher in charge,
and Jesse Lee, Presiding Elder. There were in all
New England at that time but four circuits, and one
hundred and sixty-seven members. Mr. Smith
preached but seldom in the city, devoting most of his
time and labor to other and more important parts of
the State.

Of Rev. Lemuel Smith, the first regularly appointed Methodist preacher to Rhode Island, we
have very little knowledge. He joined the traveling connection in 1788, and was sent to organize
the Cambridge circuit, N. Y. His labors on that
circuit resulted, by the blessing of God, in his returning to the next Annual Conference a membership of
one hundred and fifty-four, the most of whom
were converted during the year. The work spread
through all that section of the State of New York,
and to the frontier towns of Vermont. In 1789 he was
the colleague of the excellent Peter Moriarty, on the

New Rochelle circuit. In 1790 he was on the New Lebanon circuit, N. Y., with Thomas Everard. In 1791 he was sent to Hartford, Conn., with the eccentric, afterwards apostate, Rainer. In 1792 he traveled the first circuit in Rhode Island. The next year (1763) he traveled the Litchfield circuit with the eloquent and indomitable Ostrander. In 1794 he was on the Tolland circuit with George Pickering. In 1795 he travels the Granville circuit with Zebulon Kankey. The next year he located, and like many a man of promise in those days, is heard of no more. Where he lived, and how he died, we have failed to learn. While in the work he was a successful minister of the word; but like many good men in those days, was under the necessity of retiring from the itinerant work for want of an adequate support.

In 1793 Providence was connected with the Greenwich circuit; David Kendall and Enoch Mudge, preachers; Ezekiel Cooper, Presiding Elder.

REV. JAMES WILSON IS SETTLED IN PROVIDENCE.

It was during this year that Rev. James Wilson was settled over the Broad Street Congregational Church of this city, as colleague of Rev. Joseph

Snow, before mentioned. Mr. Wilson's relation to
Methodism, and especially of the Methodism of Providence, deserves a brief notice in this place. He was
a Palatine; born in the city of Limerick, Ireland,
1760. His mother was the daughter of the famous
Philip Guier, one of Mr. Wesley's most devoted
and successful preachers. He was awakened and
led to Christ under the labors of the famous Samuel
Bradburn, and soon after became a member of the
Wesleyan Society. In 1783 Mr. Wesley, pleased
with his gifts, sent him to the Limerick circuit. He
soon became a probationer in the Irish Conference;
but marrying before the term of his probation had
expired, he was returned to the local ranks, as no
man was allowed to marry while on probation. His
offense being not a moral, but merely an ecclesiastical
one, he remained in the connection, and maintained
his standing among his brethren. He entered into
business, and failing to succeed, took passage in a
ship commanded by a Mr. Warner, bound for America. He arrived in Providence, May 27, 1791. On
his arrival he was recommended by Capt. Warner to
the favorable notice of his friends, by whom he was
invited to preach in a private house in the evening.
This was his first introduction into Providence, the

place which was to be the field of his labors for nearly half a century. Mr. Wilson went South, and for a time preached in Baltimore, in connection with Rev. William Hammett. Why he did not enter the American Methodist connection at that time is not known. He returned North, and in October 1793, was ordained as Mr. Snow's colleague. Mr. Wilson did not long maintain the most happy relations with Mr. Snow, for in less than two years Mr. Snow with many of his members withdrew, and formed what is now the Richmond Street Church, leaving Mr. Wilson 28 members—8 males and 20 females. The poverty of the church—being so greatly reduced in numbers—rendered it necessary for Mr. Wilson to teach school in order to secure a support.

Mr. Wilson having been a Methodist preacher, necessarily drew around him most of those whose sympathies were in that direction, and he hoped no doubt, to absorb that element in the community, and render it unnecessary, if not impossible for Methodism to be established in the town. We can in no other way explain his opposition to Methodism, which we shall have occasion to notice; and in fact, he has been heard to say as much.

In 1794 Providence was still connected with the

Greenwich circuit; Joseph Lovell, preacher; George Roberts, Presiding Elder.

In 1795 John Hill and Daniel Bromley, preachers; Jesse Lee, Presiding Elder.

In 1796 Stephen Hull, preacher; Jesse Lee, Presiding Elder.

In 1797 Nathaniel Chapin and Wesley Budd. Some of these names are familiar to American Methodism. They were heroic men in our early Itinerancy.

PROVIDENCE A STATION.—JOSHUA HALL.

In 1798 Providence appears on the minutes for the first time as a Station—Joshua Hall, preacher in charge. George Pickering, Presiding Elder.

Mr. Hall supported himself chiefly by teaching a small private school, on what was then known as "Tanyard Lane"—now Deane Street. He preached in private houses, in the town house, and in fact, wherever a door was opened.

July 26th of this year, Bishop Asbury passed through Providence, on his way from Gen. Lippet's to Warren, but does not stop to preach.

REV. MR. WILSON'S OPPOSITION TO METHODISM.

Rev. Mr. Wilson had been induced, from some

cause, we know not what, unless it be the presence of a stationed Methodist preacher in town, to publish a book against Methodism, entitled, "Apostolic Church Government displayed, and the Government and system of the Methodist Episcopal Church Investigated," &c. It was a book of no special merit, and produced no very great impression on the public mind. While Mr. Asbury was in Warren, Jesse Lee, who was present, read to him portions of Mr. Wilson's work. Of it Mr. Asbury remarks; "It appears to be the language of two or three men; who they are, I know not; but be they who they may, they are mild without merit, and in some things are very simple, if not silly." The book has long since disappeared.

FIRST CLASS ORGANIZED.

November 4th, of this year, Mr. Hall organized the first Methodist Class in Providence. It was formed, says Amy Remington, who was one of the number, at the house of Mr. Ostrander, on Chestnut Street. Who this Mr. Ostrander was, I have failed to learn.

The class was composed of five persons, viz., Shubal Cady,—leader, Annie Cady, Amey Remington, Martha Clark and Mehitable Potter. Some have added Diadama Tripp and Rebecca Burk. But after a very careful examination of the matter, I am satisfied that they were not members of that first class, at the time of its organization, but were added very soon after it was formed. The members of that first class have all passed away.

Joshua Hall, who has the honor of forming the first class in Providence, was a man of marked ability. He had few superiors in the pulpit. I shall never forget his godly counsels and fatherly assistance, when a boy preacher, I traveled the circuit where he resided ; nor shall I forget the last sermon I heard him preach, (then more than eighty years of age) which for finish and brilliancy I have seldom heard equaled. From beginning to end it was an unbroken string of pearls.

Mr. Hall was somewhat distinguished in the political world, and for a time was acting Governor of the State of Maine. He died December 25th, 1862, aged ninety-four years ; having preached the gospel seventy years.

Rhode Island Methodism owes much, under God, to Joshua Hall. Some of her most prosperous churches were organized by him.

The members of that first class deserve special notice. They have all passed away, and no special record of them remains, except the five Methodist churches which have sprung from that little seed; a church for each original member of the society. They were brave, hopeful and pious. Hearts less strong had been crushed by the opposition which met them on all sides. They defended their faith single-handed and alone, until God sent them helpers, and with them prosperity.

SHUBAL CADY.

Mr. Cady, the only male member and Leader of the first class, was a man of sterling worth, and well qualified for such a work. He was born in Killingly, Conn., May 5, 1769. The date and place of his conversion are not given. He came to Providence in 1791, and was united in marriage, not long after, to Miss Anna Earl. Of Mrs. Cady's character and death we have but very little information. She was a lady of remarkably frail constitution, and possessed of that peculiar nervous temperament which is sometimes confounded with irritability, and not unfrequently judged of incorrectly. Rev. Alex. M'Clain used to call her,—with how much justice we are unable to judge,—"Bro. Cady's little wasp." She is said to have been a lady of devout piety. She was one of the original members of the class, but did not long survive its formation. Her death occurred about the year 1806. Such was her natural feebleness that she could not have been very active in the society. She died in peace, and was the first member of the class to be gathered to the Church triumphant.

In 1808, while attending a Quarterly Meeting in Portsmouth, R. I., Mr. Cady made the acquaintance of Mrs. Wait Tinkham, of Freetown, Mass., then engaged in school teaching in Portsmouth. She was introduced to him by the Quakers, who were numerous in town, as the "Praying Woman." With this recommendation Mr. Cady was well pleased; and through all her subsequent life she proved herself worthy of the Quaker title. Few women of her day gave evidence of stronger faith, or of more intimate communion with God. Her prayers were mighty through God, for she knew in whom she had believed.

Mr. Cady's father,—David Cady,—residing in the same house, was a most rigid Baptist, and not at all friendly to the Methodists. So bitter was his oppo-

ition that it was not pleasant for preachers to sto p
at the house.   But frequently at night, Mr. Cady
and his good wife would let down from their cham-
ber window, bed and bedding to be taken to Mrs.
Remington's, or Tripp's, for the accommodation of the
Circuit Preachers, and not unfrequently food went
with the couch. Mr. Cady was a man of faith.
The following incident is related of him :   Mr. Bar-
stow, of Providence, was in his bake-shop arranging
his oven, when, under powerful conviction and awakening, he fell, and cried loudly for mercy.   One and
another came in and prayed for him, but without any
relief to his mind, until Mr. Cady came in, knelt by
his side and began to pray, when he was almost in-
stantly converted to God.   Those who remember
him in Providence testify to his uncommon zeal and
Christian activity.

In the year 1812 Mr. Cady left Providence, and
removed to Killingly, his native town, and for a time
was engaged in tavern keeping.   But being a strong
temperance man, and feeling that he could not deal
in ardent spirits, and that such a house could not be
maintained in those times on strict temperance pr in-
ciples, he abandoned the business, sold out, and re-

3

moved to Griswold, Conn., where he spent the remainder of his life.

No sooner had he become settled in his new home, than his ardent spirit, in connection with his "praying" wife, sought to establish there the means of grace. They first invited their neighbors to come in and sing with them ; then to unite in prayer ; then to seek the Lord. Many were the souls converted through the labors of these earnest Methodist Christians.

Mr. Cady was an invalid, and a very great sufferer, for about twenty of the last years of his life. But in all his sufferings he kept up the old Methodist practice of reading the word of God, prayer, and fasting. He "did not live by bread alone." He was one of those Christians who believed in the power of God to slay and to make alive. He departed this life in Griswold, July, 1842, in the seventy-third year of his age, having been a follower of Christ for more than fifty years. Methodism in Providence owes much to the irreproachable character, constant faith and burning zeal of Shubal Cady, its first Class Leader. Peace to his memory.

AMEY REMINGTON.

Mrs. Remington was a lady occupying a high social position, being connected with one of the first families of the State. She was the daughter of William and Elizabeth Jones, born in Newport R. I., March 26, 1750. She was the sister of Hon. William Jones, once Governor of Rhode Island, and grandfather of Ex. Gov. Dyer, still living. She married (at what date I am unable to learn) Capt. Remington, by whom she had two children, John and Peleg. John was a seafaring man. He sailed from Philadelphia, took the small pox, and died. Peleg resided in Warwick. Capt. Remington did not survive many years after his marriage, but died, leaving his wife in very moderate circumstances. But, being a person of an enterprising character, Mrs. Remington resorted to school teaching, and whatever else she could do for a livelihood. She lived to the advanced age of eighty years, and departed this life at the residence of her son, Peleg, in Warwick, April 13, 1830. Her remains were brought to Providence, and she was buried from the residence of her brother, No. 270 Westminster Street, and her remains now lie in the beautiful cemetery at Swan Point, waiting the call of the last trump, which shall summon her to the possession of that kingdom for which she so ardently labored.

Mrs. Remington was a lady of no ordinary ability. From what I have been able to learn of her character, she was a person of positive convictions, of ardent temperament, and unwavering faith. Though connected with one of the first families of the State, she joyfully united her religious destiny with a people then everywhere spoken against, and cheerfully bore her portion of whatever reproach fell on them. The first class met in her house, on Chestnut Street, where they prayed for and encouraged each other to hold fast their faith. Her house was the common resort of the members, a kind of rallying point for the little band, where they talked over socially their prospects and discouragements. These early toils and labors were the theme upon which she delighted to dwell in later years. There is no doubt that early Methodism in Providence owes very much to the earnest labors and consistent faith of Amey Remington. She was the leading female member of that brave band, and well and ably did she defend and illustrate the doctrines she had espoused.

MEHITABLE POTTER.

Miss Potter was one of the immortal five. She was a quiet, unassuming Christian lady. Less intellectual and prominent than her associates, but not less humble and devout. She died May 1, 1847.

MARTHA CLARK.

She was born in Providence, August 21, 1773, and was about twenty-five years of age when the first class was organized. At what time, or under whose labors she experienced religion, we have no information, only that she became a Christian quite young. She was a lady of more than ordinary ability, both natural and acquired. During the latter years of her life she devoted much time to writing and publishing small tracts. One, entitled "The Victims of Amusements," exhibited no little ability. She was regarded by all who knew her as an estimable Christian lady. In her last days, for some cause, she became somewhat desponding; but, at the close of her protracted life, her faith triumphed over all doubt, and she departed to her rest in great peace, September 5, 1858, aged eighty-five.

She died at the house of her step-sister, Mrs. Thomas Fletcher. She was never married.

Martha Clark was the last of the original class. She lived to see the faith which she embraced in early life, when it was everywhere spoken against, triumph gloriously. The little one had become a thousand. Her funeral services were attended by Rev. Joseph Snelling, the first Methodist minister to administer the ordinances of religion to the little band, of which Martha Clark was an honored member. On the whole, for intelligence, zeal for the salvation of souls, and unshaken faith in God, the equal of that first class is seldom found. The fact that they all held fast their faith unto the end, under such a storm of persecution as they endured, is quite remarkable. They "all died in faith," some "not having received the promise, but having seen it afar off, were persuaded of it, and embraced it, and confessed that they were pilgrims and strangers," and were seeking a "better country."

In 1799 Providence was connected with Warren and Greenwich,—Ezekiel Canfield, Joshua Hall, and Freeman Bishop were the preachers; George Pickering, Presiding Elder.

In 1800 the circuit remained unchanged. The preachers were Joseph Snelling and Solomon Langdon.

On the 14th of July, of this year, Bishop Asbury, accompanied by Bishop Whatcoat, passed through Providence, but made no stop; Bishop Asbury remarking, " The time is not yet come."

In 1801 the circuit was unchanged. It was connected with Boston District, Joshua Taylor, Presiding Elder; John Finnegan and Daniel Fidler, Circuit Preachers.

BAPTISM FIRST ADMINISTERED.

May 1st of this year, Rev. Joseph Snelling administered the ordinance of baptism to Diadama Tripp; it being the first baptism by the Methodists in Providence.

THE FIRST COMMUNION.

There are conflicting statements as to when and where the first communion service was held. One authority says; August 28th of this year, the sacrament of the Lord's Supper was administered by Rev. John Finnegan, the preacher in charge, at the house of Diadama Tripp, to twelve persons, five males and seven females. This is said to have been the first instance in which the Lord's Supper was administered by the Methodists in this town.

Another authority, still living (1868), and claiming to have been present at the first communion, describes it as follows : " The first communion service was held in the Court House. The preachers present were Joseph Snelling and John Finnegan. The table was arranged in the centre of the room, with glass tumblers and an earthen plate for the bread, and a common glass decanter for the wine. There was quite a number present, some of whom were from out of town. To me it was a memorable time. I was quite young, and had not made a profession of religion. After all the members had partaken, the preacher invited those who felt their need of Christ, and were resolved to seek him with the whole heart, to come. No one started. I felt my need of Christ, and felt that I ought to go. I ventured alone—walked the length of the room, and knelt at the table. In a moment I felt that Jesus died for me. I felt that he approved the act, and comforted and strengthened me as I had never been before." *

It is quite certain that this was the second communion service held by the Methodists in this town, and that the one before referred to did take

* Sarah J. Randall, Worcester, Mass.

place at the time and place named. Our authority is Amey Remington, one of the members of the first class, who was doubtless present on the occasion.

In 1802 the preachers were Reuben Hubbard, Caleb Morris, and Allen H. Cobb.

In 1803 Providence is. an extensive circuit. Alex. McLane and Noble W. Thomas are the preachers; George Pickering, Presiding Elder.

THE FIRST QUARTERLY MEETING.

August 12th and 13th of this year, the first Quarterly Meeting, so much prized by the early Methodists, was held in this town. It was held, as were most of their public meetings at this time, in the Town House. The Presiding Elder, Rev. George Pickering, preached on the occasion, and administered the Sacrament. It was a memorable season. The society was greatly encouraged, and the prospect before them seemed more hopeful.

TOWN HOUSE.

The Town House, so often referred to, in which the early Methodist preachers preached, was an old Congregational church, corner of College and Benefit Streets, which had been purchased by the town for a

Town House. It was used by all denominations not having churches.

In 1804 the preachers were Asa Pattie, D. Burge, and Clement Parker.

DR. COKE VISITS PROVIDENCE.

It was during this year that Dr. Coke, the first Bishop of the Methodist Episcopal Church, and the first Protestant Bishop of the New World, visited Providence. He landed at Newport, from New York, June, 1804. From Newport he came to Bristol, where he was entertained by Capt. William Pearce, known as Father Pearce. The rector of the Episcopal Church, after being satisfied that the Doctor had been Episcopally ordained, was a Presbyter of the English Church, a graduate of Oxford, and a Doctor of Law, consented that he should preach in the Episcopal Church, on the further condition that Capt. Pearce should blow out the candles at the close of the service, it being the first evening service ever held in the church. Father Pearce conveyed the Doctor from Bristol to Providence in a small packet. A gentleman in New York had requested James Burrill, Esq., a lawyer and highly respectable citizen of Providence, to receive Dr.

Coke with the regards due an English Bishop. Rev.
Thomas Lyell, then stationed in Newport, accompanied the Bishop to Providence. A crowd were assembled on the wharf to see and welcome an English Bishop; among them, Shubal Cady, the class
leader, who had no thought of doing more than get
a look at the man whose fame was world wide. Arrangements had been made for the Doctor's enter-
tainment at the palatial residence of John Enos
Clark, Esq., a wealthy citizen of Providence; and
his carriage was in waiting at the wharf. As the
Doctor landed, he inquired of Messrs. Clark and
Burrill if there were any Methodists in town. They
shook their heads, and remarked that they knew of
none. Mr. Cady, hearing the question and answer,
stepped forward and said, "There is a small class
here, but not much known," and at the same time
introduced to the Doctor Mr. Benjamin Turpin, at
whose house the preachers were accustomed to stop.
The Doctor inquired where the circuit preachers
stopped when they came to town, and being informed that they usually stopped at Mr. Turpin's, he
expressed a desire to stop there too, if convenient;
and being assured that it would be very gratifying to
the family to have him do so, though in compara-

tively humble circumstances, Mr. Clark's carriage conveyed him to Mr. Turpin's residence, on the southwest corner of High and Stewart Streets. The house is still standing.

Dr. Coke remained in Providence one week, spending one day in Boston during the time. He was preparing his Commentary at the time, and devoted a portion of each day to that work. He was invited to preach in several of the churches in town. He inquired where the Circuit Preachers preached when they came to town, and being informed that they usually preached in the old Town House, he refused all invitations to preach elsewhere, until he had first preached there. He knew that the Methodists in Providence were feeble, despised and persecuted, and he was anxious that whatever influence he possessed should be turned to their account.

Dr. Coke spent one Sabbath in Providence, preaching morning and evening in Rev. Mr. Wilson's church. He is said, by one who heard him, to have preached with great power. The Doctor had known Mr. Wilson favorably as a Methodist preacher in Ireland, and Mr. Wilson held the Doctor in high esteem.

The evening after Dr. Coke and Mr. Lyell arrived, they performed a religious ceremony which may somewhat astonish us. A number of the members of the class were present to witness the ceremony, which consisted in the "washing of feet," after the Apostolic practice. They were assembled in Mr. Turpin's parlor. Mr Lyell called for a basin of water. Dr. Coke sat in his chair with his eyes closed, and his hands clasped. Mr. Lyell knelt before him, and proceeded to wash the Doctor's feet, purely as a religious ceremony. At the close, Dr. Coke prayed; and, says one who was present, "The blessing that came to my heart in answer to that prayer I have not lost to this day." (1868.) This may be regarded as an illustration of the Apostolic simplicity of these holy men.

At another time, Rev. Mr. Wilson and a number of friends being present, Mr. Wilson requested the Doctor to relate a vision which he once had, and of which Mr. Wilson had knowledge in the old country. The Doctor did not seem very much inclined to do it, remarking that he seldom referred to it, but, if they desired him to relate it he would not object; and proceeded to do so. He arose from his chair, clasped his hands, and said in a very impressive manner that he was once very sick, and finally supposed by his

4

friends to be dead. He felt that angels took him away from earth, and as they bore him towards heaven he seemed to be passing through waves of glory which forced him back. He wished his attendants to carry him immediately into the presence of Mr. Wesley. But, as they approached the gates of the city, he was stopped and informed by the angels that he could not enter now, but must return to earth for a season. At this announcement he felt regret, such as he had never before known. "Must I return?" he inquired. Being assured that that was God's will, he replied: "If I must go back, let me go and blaze until I die." In that moment his recovery commenced, and it is not too much to say of Dr. Coke, that he did "blaze" until death.

Mr. Turpin's house, during Dr. Coke's visit there, was thronged most of the time with Methodists from different parts of the circuit, to whom he gave earnest exhortations, and for whom he offered fervent prayers.

Rev. Mr. Lyell, who accompanied Dr. Coke to Providence, preached in the afternoon of the Sabbath a memorable sermon on the sacrifice of Isaac. Mr. Lyell was a man of uncommon ability. He is said to have been the Summerfield of his times. He

joined the traveling connection in 1791. In 1797,
while pastor of the old Light Street Church, Baltimore, he was elected chaplain to Congress, under the
administration of the elder Adams; and was the first
Methodist preacher elected to that office. In 1802
and 1803, he was stationed in Boston with Rev.
Epaphras Kibby. A most remarkable revival attended their labors. He was next sent to Newport
for three months, after which he located. He subsequently joined the Protestant Episcopal Church, and
at the time of his death (1850) was Rector of
Christ's Church, New York. He was a good man,
and retained his love for his old associates to the end.
Mr. Benjamin Turpin, at whose house Dr. Coke was
entertained, was a Quaker, but had forfeited his
membership by marrying out of the society. He
was never a member of the Methodist Church, but
he loved the early Methodist preachers, and his
house was the common preaching place for many
years. Mrs. Turpin was a member of Mr. Wilson's
church until her triumphant death, which occurred in
1843. She used to say that she loved the very name
of Methodist. She was often visited by Mr. Wilson
and members of his church, and urged not to give
her influence in favor of the Methodists; but she

modestly replied that she felt it her duty to stand by the Methodists. Few families in Providence aided the cause of Methodism more than Mr. Turpins', though neither he nor his wife were members.

In 1805 Rev. Epaphras Kibby was appointed to Providence. He remained but a part of the year, and left, for two reasons, viz. : feebleness of health, and, as he informed Hezekiah Anthony, because he was "tired of preaching to bare walls."

In 1806 Providence was a large circuit again, connected with the New London District, Thomas Branch, Presiding Elder; Pliny Pratt and Joseph Smith, circuit preachers.

These were dark days for the cause of Methodism in Providence ; but God sustained the few. There were many members of Rev. Mr. Wilson's church who were not only ardent lovers, but firm supporters of Methodism. Among them were Mrs. Turpin, before named, Nathaniel Fuller, Thomas Young and others. Mr. Fuller was a most devout lover of Methodism. Mr. Young was an artist, and possessing some wealth, was able to render material aid to the cause.

Liscomb Fuller united with the society about this time, and succeeded Shubal Cady as Class leader.

He was a valuable man, and for years served faithfully the cause of Methodism. David Cady, brother of Shubal, was a valuable acquisition to the church. He was a good man, and when he prayed for fire, as he often did, he became a man mighty through God. The society held their meetings, chiefly at Mr. Turpins', Liscomb Fuller's, Amey Remington's, and the Town House.

In 1807, John Tinkham, preacher; Elijah R. Sabin, Presiding Elder.

JESSE LEE'S LAST VISIT TO PROVIDENCE.

In 1808 Benjamin P. Hill was preacher in charge. It was during this year that Jesse Lee made his last visit to Providence. He left Baltimore on the 31st of May, for New England, having been absent about eight years. He arrived at Gen. Lippett's—his old friend—in Cranston, Saturday the 10th of July. Here he spent the Sabbath, preached twice, and administered the Lord's Supper; and had, he says, "another precious time of the love and presence of God." Tuesday, 12th, "I rode to Providence and put up at John Lippett's, and at night preached in the Town House. I believe some good was done at that time, and I hope the fruit thereof will be seen after many days. It has been many years since I preached in this town; but I felt something of the same union with the people that I formerly felt. There is a small society in Providence."

Early the next day he left for Bristol and Newport; and his voice is heard in Providence no more. Eight years later, 1816, Sept. 12th, at the house of Mr. Seller's, Hillsboro', Md., he died, shouting "Glory! glory! glory! hallelujah! Jesus reigns!" He was buried in the city of Baltimore, where his mortal remains still rest.

In 1809 Providence and Smithfield are united. Greenleaf R. Norris and Pliny Brett are the circuit preachers; Elijah Hedding, Presiding Elder.

In 1810, P. Brett and Elisha Streeter.

In 1811, P. Brett and S. Wingate; Joel Winch, Presiding Elder.

In 1812, Benjamin Sabine.

During these years the little class, formed by Mr. Hall, met, chiefly at the house of Amey Remington. They sung and prayed and hoped for better times; but it was "hope against hope." They were regarded as an insignificant band of wild fanatics, who must soon disappear. But they knew "in whom they had believed."

In 1813 Providence was united with East Greenwich circuit. Daniel Wentworth and W. Banister
were the preachers.

ABBY BRENTON MUMFORD.

We should do injustice to the history of Methodism
in Providence, did we not pause here a moment to
notice one of the most intelligent and devoted of all
the members of the society at this time,—Abby
Brenton Mumford. She was the daughter of Wm.
Brenton, of Newport, R. I., an historic name in that
ancient city. She is said to have been a lady of superior education, great refinement of manners, of
deep, constant piety, and uncommon devotion to
God. She was indeed a brilliant light in the church
of her choice. Her influence was felt, not only in
the society, but everywhere. Not only her voice but
her pen was employed to set forth the excellency of
the Saviour, who had saved her to the uttermost.
She was unfortunate in her marriage ; her husband
becoming a hopeless inebriate, she became very much
reduced in her circumstances, and was forced to de-
pend upon her own exertions for the support of herself and three children. She received aid occasionally from Mrs. Thomas Ives, a schoolmate, to whom

she was ardently attached. Others aided her more
or less, so that real want she never knew. When
Dr. Coke visited Providence, she became so deeply
interested in his conversation and spirit that she could
not be deprived the privilege of spending the time at
Mr. Turpin's. She is said to have begged the privilege of stopping with the family while Dr. Coke
remained, that she might enjoy his conversation and
prayers. This favor was cheerfully granted, and
no week of her life was to her of greater spiritual
profit.

She was beloved by all who knew her, and revered
as one of the brightest examples of exalted piety,
combined with superior intelligence and womanly
modesty.

She departed this life in great peace, August 5th,
1814, in the 41st year of her age.

It is doubtful if any of the members of the church
now living have any distinct remembrance of her.
It is due that this brief record of her Christian character should be made. She was the grandmother of
Mrs. George M. Butts, of Providence.

OTHER NAMES.

Three sisters, Sarah, Mary and Nancy Allen, from

Greenwich, joined the little band about this time.
They were devoted, earnest Christian ladies, and gave
all their influence in favor of Methodism. Sarah
taught school, Mary and Nancy worked at some
trade. Subsequently Sarah became the wife of
Joshua Soule, for many years one of the Bishops of
the Methodist Episcopal Church; but who, at the
time of the great pro-slavery secession in 1844,
united his fortunes with the slave power, and went
South. He has recently passed to his reward. Mary
and Nancy subsequently went South to reside with
the Bishop.

In 1814 Providence was a part of the East Greenwich circuit, Joel Steele, preacher in charge.

Up to this time the circuit preachers visited Providence but seldom. It was unproductive soil. They
preached in the Town House and in private houses,
and wherever they could find an open door. It
seemed very doubtful if the seed sown by Garrettson, Lee, Asbury, Hall and others, would ever pro-
duce permanent fruit. But God watched the seed.

In the year 1811 or 1812, Mr. John Sutcliff and
Samuel Greenhalgh came to reside in Providence.
They were earnest Christian men, and Methodists.
They urged upon the society the importance of hav-

ing some place of worship, however small, which
they could control.

They succeeded in hiring a small school-house, situated on what is now known as Middle St., but called
in the classic language of those times, " Cat Alley."
The building is still standing (1866), and may be
seen in the rear of Mitchell & Magoon's, Broad St.,

It is a remarkable fact, that in nearly all our
large cities, Methodism was cradled in a hovel. It
worshiped in some alley, or by-place, quite unob-
served by the more wealthy and honorable. But of
this we ought not to be ashamed, when we remember
that the Lawgiver of Israel was a slave child, res-
cued from a rush ark in the Nile ; and the Saviour of
the world was born in a stable.

From 1811 to 1815, there was preaching in this
little school-house once in two weeks, on week day
evenings, but seldom, or never, on the Sabbath.

In the fitting up of this school-house, the members
of the society were taxed to their utmost ability.
Rebecca Burke informed the writer that she contributed the last twenty dollars she possessed toward fur-

nishing seats. Such sacrifices give evidence of their deep interest in the cause.

In 1815 Providence was connected with Mansfield circuit. Orlando Hinds and F. Dane were the preachers. But it does not appear that they visited Providence often. Everything seemed to be at the lowest possible ebb.

THE FIRST REVIVAL.

Rev. Van Rensselaer Osborn, who was traveling the Needham circuit, having business in Bristol, passed through Providence, and on Wednesday evening preached in the little school house. Returning from Bristol on Saturday, he consented to remain and preach on the Sabbath. The congregation was not large—only about twenty-five or thirty—but it was God's time to work. In the midst of the forenoon sermon two young ladies of some note in the town, became powerfully awakened, and cried aloud for mercy,—a new thing in Providence. The news of this strange phenomenon spread with great rapidity through the town, so that in the afternoon, the little house which would accommodate only about one hundred and fifty persons, was crowded; and in the evening, so great had become the excitement, there was no room to receive the people, "no, not so much as about the door; and the power of the Lord was present to heal."

Mr. Osborn went to his circuit, spent a short time with his people, and returned to Providence. The work had now become so general that there seemed to be an imperative demand for his labors here. A petition was addressed to the Presiding Elder, Rev. Asa Kent, urging him to permit Mr. Osborn to take charge of the work. He came contrary to the wishes of the Presiding Elder, and became pastor of the church, Sept. 14th, 1815, and for doing so his character was arrested at the following Conference, but he was successfully defended by Rev. George Pickering.

The society numbered at this time thirty-three members. They were all poor, but they were full of faith and the Holy Ghost. Theirs was no unruffled sea. They encountered the most violent opposition; but under the leadership of Mr. Osborn their labors were crowned with remarkable success. "We were beaten down," says Mr. Osborn, "by every person that could lift a club against us. The popular opinion was that the Methodists were the offscouring of all things."

Their situation was exceedingly unfavorable for
gathering a society. "Another advantage which
other denominations had over us was," says Mr. Osborn, "we had only this little school-room. It was
therefore sounded through the town that we were like
the crackling of thorns under a pot, and that in one
year not one of us would be found. 'See,' said the
multitude, 'they have no house, and they are so poor
that they cannot build one.'"

By these methods the society was deprived of large
numbers of members who were awakened and converted at their meetings. "Seven young men at
one time," says Mr. Osborn, "were telling their experience at the Baptist Church; one after another
testified that they were awakened at the Methodist
meeting, until at last the preacher arose and said, "I
do not want you to tell where you were awakened,
nor when, nor by whom; tell that you are, that is
enough." "I was credibly informed," continues Mr.
Orborn, "by a member of the Baptist Church, that
she had heard fifty persons relate their experience, all
of whom dated their seriousness from our meetings."
During that revival the Baptists received about

5

eighty members, and the Methodists only about sixty.

SACRIFICES.

There were no sacrifices, even under these circumstances, which the society was not ready to make to sustain the gospel among them. Mr. Osborn says: "Many orphan girls gave weekly a sum, which in the aggregate, amounted to from six to twelve dollars a year; and brethren who earned their bread by days' labor gave six, twelve and twenty-five dollars a year." When we consider the small pay received by day laborers in those times, these are remarkable contributions.

THE FIRST MEETING HOUSE.

A suitable house of worship, one which would accommodate the people, seemed to the minister and the society an indispensable necessity. But how to procure the means they knew not.

Mr. Osborn drew up a subscription paper, and called upon all the principal men in the town, securing what they were pleased to give for the object, and then "I called," he says, "on every one I met." The result of this effort was $500.00 raised for a new church. With this sum raised, a carpenter was employed, and the work of erecting the first Methodist Church in Providence commenced. The house was completed and dedicated to God, Sunday, June 1st, 1816; sermon by the pastor, Rev. V. R. Osborn.

The house stood on the southeast corner of Aborn and Washington Streets. It still stands on the same spot, and is occupied for a dwelling-house.

We will not attempt to describe the delight experienced by the struggling society at the completion of this their first temple.

THE CLOSE OF MR. OSBORN'S FIRST YEAR.

Thursday of the following week, Mr. Osborn left for Conference—held that year in Bristol. He left in the society 99 whites and 12 blacks; in all, 111, including a few at Pawtucket. This was a great work to be accomplished in eight months. But the work was not complete.

Mr. Osborn was returned to Providence the following year. On his return he found financial matters, to use his own words, "in a most distressing state." He left at once for New York, Philadelphia and Baltimore to collect funds for the relief of the society. After some weeks' absence he returned with

$800.00. "This," he says, "settled our creditors for a season."

FIRST QUARTERLY CONFERENCE.

It was during the latter part of August, or the first of September, that the first Quarterly Conference was held in the chapel, and the first in Providence of which we have any record. Rev. Asa Kent was Presiding Elder, and Rev. V. R. Osborn, Preacher in charge. The Class Leaders at this time were, Samuel Greenhalgh, Henry Adams, Robert McFarling, and Hezekiah Briggs. The first board of Stewards appointed by this Conference were, Lowell Adams, Henry Adams, Daniel Keen, and Liscomb Fuller.

Lowell Adams was elected first Secretary of the society, and Henry Adams the first District Steward. They adjourned to meet Nov. 27th, 1816.

FREE CHURCH EXPERIMENT FAILS.

Mr. Osborn had been sanguine from the first that a free church could be sustained here; that a congregation could be best collected by free seats, and that the poor would be better provided for. But their house, he says, "soon became a rendezvous for everything that was bad."

To remedy this evil, as they had no laws to protect them, they changed their seats into pews and rented them. They reserved enough for the poor, or those unable to hire, and rented the remainder for six months for $240.00.

About this time many of the society, on account of the severity of the times, were obliged to leave the town and seek employment elsewhere.

During the year 10 were expelled, 15 removed and 2 died. With those at Pawtucket not included, there were but 47 regular members in society, and many of these were expecting soon to leave.

FIRST SUNDAY SCHOOL.

Mr. Osborn was the first to organize a Sunday School and look after the interests of the children. " I resolved," he says, " to do what I could for the children of the little congregation that I had collected. I therefore, in the latter part of the year 1815, formed a Sabbath School and put it in operation, according to the best of my means."

THE COLORED PEOPLE.

He interested himself for the colored people of the

town. "They were," he says, "in a deplorable situation. They had no place of worship, nor was there a congregation in town which desired their attendance." He opened a school for them, taught them two nights in the week and preached to them a third, all gratuitously.

MR. OSBORN CLOSES HIS LABORS IN PROVIDENCE.

Mr. Osborn's labors with this church were greatly owned of God. He came feeling that God called him. He yielded to his impressions, he tells us, contrary to his own interests, and the judgment of his Presiding Elder. He took the entire responsibility in building the church. He saw dark and trying times. "Sometimes," he says, "I wished I had never seen Providence; at other times I rejoiced greatly at the work of God; however, I never have been truly sorry."

During the first year he bore all his expenses, furnished his own clothes, and paid $50.00 towards his board, and received at the Conference $32.00.

The second year he received about $55.00 from the charge, while his expenses were $4.50 per week.

The society being poor, he entertained nearly all visitors and strangers, so that his expenses during the year were about $300. He sold his horse and saddle and a part of his library to meet these expenses, and left the town about $200.00 in debt, which he afterward paid by teaching school.

On leaving the charge he makes this record : "The Lord will bless this little flock, for their hearts are open to do more than is in their power; and I bear them witness that I leave them little and humble; and if it were posssible they would pluck out their very eyes and give them me. May the Lord ever keep them humble and little in their own eyes, and prosper them, and may I, V. Rensselear Osborn, meet them in heaven."

Mr. Osborn was received into the New England Conference in 1813, at the age of 22 ; having traveled under the Presiding Elder about two years. His health failing, and being unwilling to be considered burdensome to the church, he asked and received a location in 1823. He spent his time chiefly in teaching in Manchester, Conn., and Baltimore, Md., until 1843 ; his health improving he was re-admitted into the Providence Conference, and continued to labor with much success until 1846, when he "ceased at once to work and live." He died in Manchester, Conn., Sabbath morning, Nov. 29th, 1846, at 4 1-2 o'clock, at the age of 56. At the time of his death he was engaged in a gracious revival. God had crowned his efforts with remarkable success. On the previous Sabbath, Nov. 22, he had preached with remarkable success. On the same evening he was taken with a violent attack of lung fever, and inflammation of the bowels. For four days he suffered much, but on the 5th mortification took place, and on the following Sabbath he entered into his rest.

Death did not find him unprepared. "I feel," he said, "a calm, sweet sinking into the will of God. I feel that all is well." When asked if his mind was peaceful, he quickly replied, "O yes!" To his daughter, standing by his bed-side, he said, "Get into the chariot, and it is a short road to the New Jerusalem. At one time he supposed himself in heaven, and began to speak of the company there,— of Moses and the prophets. Some one aroused him, and inquired if all was well. He replied, "O, yes, I am sinless now." Soon after he fell asleep. Thus ended the mortal career of one who did more, under God, than any other man, for the establishment of Methodism in Providence.

In 1817 and 1818 Rev. Solomon Sias was appointed to labor in Providence. Enoch Mudge, speaking of Mr. Sias' labors here, says, "They were exceedingly useful, both as it regards the temporal and spiritual prosperity of the church and society."

In 1819 Rev. Moses Fifield was the pastor. His labors are said to have been useful to many. About this time, on account of some trouble in Mr. Wilson's church, quite a number of the members withdrew and united with the Methodists; among them Mr. Daniel Field and his wife Zipporah. Mr. Field, being a man of considerable wealth, was a valuable acquisition to the society. Has was born 1755, and died 1830, aged 75 years. He was an uncle of the late Daniel Field, Esq., who, though not himself a member of the church, yet like his honored uncle ever manifested a deep interest in its welfare, and always contributed liberally to its support.

REV. FREEBORN GARRETTSON'S LAST VISIT TO PROVIDENCE.

It was during this year that Rev. Freeborn Garrettson visited Providence for the last time. He preached with satisfaction in the Methodist Church, and by request, in Mr. Wilson's. Eight years later this holy man, the first of our denomination to proclaim the gospel of God in this town, died in peace in the city of New York, in the 76th year of his age, and the 52d of his ministry. His last words were, "Holy holy! holy! Lord God Almighty! hallelujah! hallelujah!"

THE CHESTNUT STREET CHURCH BUILT.

In 1820 Rev. Bartholomew Otheman was appointed to this city. Few preachers have been more successful. A gracious revival commenced during Mr. Otheman's first year, and very large accessions were made to the society. The house in Aborn Street soon became too small to accommodate the crowds that flocked there to hear the word of the Lord. A more commodious house of worship was felt to be a necessity. A valuable lot, on the corner of Chestnut and Clifford Streets, was kindly donated the society by Daniel Field, Esq. A subscription was opened and contributions were made so freely that the Trustees felt themselves justified in commencing the work.

On the 6th of August, 1821, the corner-stone of the new edifice was laid with appropriate religious ceremonies. Rev. Mr. Lyon, a local preacher from New York, delivered a most eloquent address from 1 Samuel, 7 : 12, "Then Samuel took a stone and set it between Mizpeh and Shen, and called the name of it Ebenezer, saying, hitherto hath the Lord helped us." The pavilion which sheltered the orator from the rays of the morning sun, was a large umbrella, supported by Hezekiah Anthony. Rev. B. Otheman offered prayer. Bro. James Lewis laid the corner-stone. And as the early sun smiled approvingly upon this new evidence of God's favor to his church, the choir, with clear, full voices, greeted his rising with old "Victory"—

> "Now shall my head be lifted high,
>   Above my foes around;
> And songs of joy and victory
>   Within thy courts abound."

It is thought that "Old Victory" was never sung with more thrilling effect.

In five months from the time the corner stone was laid, the house was completed; and on the 1st day of January, 1822, was dedicated to the worship of Almighty God. The pastor, Rev. B. Otheman, preached the sermon on the occasion from Num. 23 : 23, "What hath God wrought?" He was assisted in the services by the Presiding Elder of the District, Rev. Erastus Otis. It is said to have been a season of refreshing from the presence of the Lord.

REV. JOHN N. MAFFITT IN PROVIDENCE.

Very soon after the society removed into the new
church, a remarkable work of God commenced under the labors of Rev. John Newland Maffitt. Never
was the capacity of this house so fully tested as during
this revival. So eager were the people to hear Mr.
Maffitt, that hours before the time of service, ladies
and gentlemen from all parts of the city would take
their stand at the door of the church, awaiting its
opening. Then, every sitting, standing and leaning
place would be occupied, and large numbers be
obliged to leave, not being able to gain admittance.

The religious excitement was not confined to the
Methodists. Episcopalians, Congregationalists, and
others, seemed, if possible, to outstrip the Methodists. The Episcopalians, especially, seem to have
monopolized Mr. Maffitt. The interest was unlike
anything ever witnessed in Providence before or since.

In 1822 Rev. T. Merritt was the pastor. This is
said, by Rev. Enoch Mudge, to have been a "year of
great and sore trials; but, by the blessing of God,
and the faithful labors of Bro. T. Merritt, the church
has been mercifully preserved and blessed."

The "trials" to which Mr. Mudge refers, grew

out of certain scandalous reports respecting the character of Mr. Maffitt.

Mr. Alex. Jones — the younger — had published, or caused to be published, in the GALAXY — a paper published in Boston, and edited by Joseph T. Buckingham — some statements, or reports, reflecting seriously on Mr. Maffitt. These published reports occasioned very great excitement. Mr. Buckingham was prosecuted for an alleged libel on the character of Mr. Maffitt, and was tried in the Municipal Court in the city of Boston, before Judge Quincy—the elder Josiah. The libel was not proved. The court gave the final decision unfavorable to Mr. Maffitt, Saturday night. Mr. Maffitt was advertised to preach on the following day in the Bromfield Street Church. The excitement was intense, and it is said that judge, jurors, lawyers and others, were present. Under the irresistible appeals of the youthful orator the whole congregation wept like children. It was generally conceded that Mr. Maffitt had conquered his defamers in the pulpit, though conquered by them at the bar. Mr. Maffitt immediately, in consequence of the decision of the court, requested that an Ecclesiastical Council might be called on his case. Accordingly a Council convened in the city of Boston, to consider the charges. Rev. Elijah Hedding was President. After investigating such facts as came before the court, the Council adjourned to Providence, to examine the depositions which were taken there. After a faithful and candid investigation of the subject, the Council were unanimous in acquitting Mr. Maffitt of the high charges alleged against him.

The Council did discover imprudence in some instances, but having received satisfactory assurances from Mr. Maffitt for the future, they express the hope that "age, experience, and divine grace will correct his faults, and make him an instrument of great good."

At the close of these investigations, Mr. Maffitt preached a memorable and exceedingly appropriate sermon in this church, from 2 Tim. 4 : 14, "Alexander the coppersmith did me much evil; the Lord reward him according to his works."

It needed such a helmsman as Timothy Merritt to guide the ship without harm in such a storm.

In 1823 and 1824 Rev. E. Mudge was stationed here. Under his ministry the church enjoyed a good degree of prosperity. He was a man greatly beloved by all who knew him. He is even now remembered by the aged members of the church, as an apostle of goodness.

It was in the month of June, of this year, that the New England Conference held its first session in Providence, in this church. Bishop George presided.

In 1825 Rev. D. Webb was stationed in Providence. For some reason he remained but one year. This year Providence reported 200 white, and 37 colored members.

In 1826 and 1827 Rev. Asa Kent was the preacher in charge. He was an uncompromising disciplinarian. He did his duty as he understood it, without regard to friend or foe. Some of the members thought his administration exceedingly severe, but no one attributed it to any other than honest motives. Providence was at this time connected with the New London District; Rev. E. H. Hyde, Presiding Elder. Providence reported at the close of Mr. Kent's term, 194 white, and 25 colored members.

In 1828 and 1829 Rev. Jacob Sanborn was pastor. Under his ministry the church enjoyed a good degree of prosperity. The membership, at the close of his term stood,—whites 200, colored 31.

In 1830 and 1831 Rev. David Kilborn was pastor.
He was a useful minister and much beloved by all.
In 1830 Providence appears as a District; Rev. J. A.
Merrill, Presiding Elder. At the close of Mr. Kilborn's term, there were reported in society 270 white,
35 colored members.

THE E. K. AVERY CASE.

In 1832 and 1833 Rev. J. Horton was the pastor. These were years of very great trial to this
church. During Mr. Horton's second year, the famous E. K. Avery case occurred, affecting not only
this, but every Methodist church in New England.
The members were more or less divided in their opinions as to the guilt or innocence of Mr. Avery. Mr.
Horton took an active part in his favor, which caused
more or less unpleasant feeling among the people.

POWER STREET CHURCH ORGANIZED.

In the latter part of the year 1832, a number of
the more enterprising members of this church, seeing
the need of a Methodist church on the east side of
the city, united in an effort which resulted in the
erection of the Power Street Church.

In 1834 Rev. J. Sanborn was again stationed in this church, and remained one year.

It was during this year that the Quarterly Conference passed and placed upon its records the following resolutions :

"Sept. 25, 1834, adopted the resolutions passed by the New England Conference, June, 1834, viz., The qualifications required of such as present themselves for admission into Conference :

1. They shall have read and studied the whole of Wesley's Sermons, together with Watson's Theological Institutes.

2. They shall be so far acquainted with the rules of English Grammar as to be able to parse in any English author.

3. Resolved, that from and after the present session of this Conference, no recommendation for the admission of any one on trial shall be considered in form, unless it specify the person's theological and literary qualifications according to the foregoing resolutions."

Members in society, — Whites 335, Colored 48.

In 1835 and 1836 Rev. A. D. Sargeant, preacher in charge.

CHESTNUT STREET CHURCH IMPROVED.

Up to this time there was very little about this meeting-house to distinguish it from a barn, — no steeple, no bell to call the people to the sacred altar, and no organ to make melody, or, as it has sometimes done, discord within. All was plain, simple, Methodistical. But at this time there was added a steeple, — not quite its present height, — a bell, and instrumental music.

COMMEND REV. A. D. SARGEANT.

Mr. Sargeant was highly esteemed by the people, if we may judge by a resolution adopted by the Quarterly Conference on his departure. They say : "We approve of the ministerial and pastoral labors of Rev. Aaron D. Sargeant during his two years service with us, and that all his duties and deportment as a Christian minister and a gentleman, have been commendable, and we part from him with regret."

In 1837 and 1838, Rev. Daniel Fillmore was pastor. Under the labors of Mr. Fillmore the church was blessed.

In 1839 and 1840 Rev. A. D. Merrill was pastor.

Father Merrill was a great favorite with the church, and beloved by all, and the work prospered in his hands.

August 21, 1840, the Preachers' Aid Society of the Providence Conference was organized in Chestnut Street Church. Rev. B. Otheman was Chairman, and Rev. A. Stevens, Secretary. This year the Providence was set off from the New England Conference.

Father Merrill leaving the charge some months before Conference, to take charge of a church in Lowell where some difficulties had arisen, Rev. W. H. Brewster was employed as a supply. He was, at the time, a member of the New Hampshire Conference, and was stationed at Haverhill, which place he left to serve this church. He was beloved by the people generally; and an earnest effort was made by the brethren to secure his transfer to the Providence Conference, and appointment to this charge. The Conference held its session in this church; it being the first session of the Providence Conference. A Committee from the church, composed of Hezekiah Anthony and others, waited on the Bishops, — Hed-

ding and Soule, — and urged Mr. Brewster's transfer as a necessity. Bishop Hedding was willing, but
Bishop Soule was inflexible.

The West Church was left to be supplied. Rev.
David Patten, Jr., of the New England Conference,
was transferred to this Conference, and stationed
here, where he remained two years. But to the
church and pastor they were years of great trial.

The refusal to appoint Mr. Brewster to the charge,
resulted in the withdrawal of about fifty members,
and the organization of the "First Wesleyan Society" formed in New England. Had Mr. Brewster been returned as was desired, very much of that
trouble might have been saved. Mr. B. became the
pastor of this offshoot, and the members, feeling that
they had been wronged on account of their views on
the subject of slavery, were not sparing in their de-
nunciations of the Mother Church.

"DORR WAR."

It was during Dr. Patten's pastorate that the first
great "American Rebellion" occurred, familiarly
known as the "Dorr War." It was bitter and
bloodless. The church, as well as the State, was
terribly rent by that political storm. But it is ad-

mitted that Dr. Patten conducted the church through that storm with a skillful hand.

In 1842 South Smithfield was connected with Providence, and Rev. George M. Carpenter was associated with Dr. Patten. Bro. Carpenter reported, as the result of his labors, one hundred conversions, and Dr. Patten about half that number. This was a good year.

REV. JOEL KNIGHT.

In 1843 Rev. Joel Knight was pastor. Bro. Knight ended his work and entered upon his reward from this charge, ceasing almost "at once to work and live." His brethren say, " He was a man of unbounded benevolence and burning zeal. Hence, in many of his appointments he met with glorious success. His last illness was very short and very painful ; but God was with him, and he triumphed gloriously, and now rests in the bosom of God."

On the death of Bro. Knight, the church being left without a pastor, Rev. Isaac S. House, a local preacher, formerly of the Illinois Conference, was invited to supply the pulpit during the year. His labors were profitable to the church.

In 1844 Rev. Thomas Ely was the pastor. Bro. Ely remained but one year.

In 1845 Rev. J. B. Husted was transferred from the New England Conference and stationed at this church.

In 1846 the names of the churches were changed from Providence West and East to Chestnut and Power Streets. Bro. Husted was returned to the charge, and it was during his pastorate that the Parsonage was built, he being the first to occupy it.

In 1847 Rev. R. W. Allen was the pastor. During Bro. Allen's second year the church became more or less affected by a number of the prominent members leaving and uniting with others from Power Street, and forming the Mathewson Street Church. Some thought this enterprise would prove highly injurious to the old church. But the opposition very soon ceased; everything assuming a hopeful aspect. A most gracious work of God followed.

REV. JAMES CAUGHEY.

Rev. James Caughey came to assist Bro. Allen in a protracted effort for a revival. He commenced his labors Dec. 3d, 1847, and continued them for three months, preaching twice each Sabbath, and four evenings during the week, and occasionally in the afternoon of week days. The work of God commenced in power, and seldom has there been witnessed a more deep, thorough, genuine work of the Spirit. Conversions among all classes were clear and satisfactory. The work was too deep to be boisterous, taking hold of the hardest hearts, and subduing the most stubborn wills. Between two and three hundred professed conversion, while hundreds were reclaimed from their backslidings. More than one hundred united with the Chestnut Street Church, and most of the others united with other Christian churches in the city.

A SPECIAL CASE.

I cannot forbear making mention of one case of great interest connected with this remarkable revival. Miss B., a young lady of high social position and extraordinary intellectual powers, belonging to a very respectable family connected with another Christian church, came to the meetings and became deeply interested in the subject of religion, and soon obtained the "pearl of great price." She was about to be married to a gentleman of wealth, and they contemplated spending some time in traveling in

foreign countries. Learning that she had become
religious, he became exceedingly offended, and demanded that she renounce her religion, or their engagement must end. He gave her a certain time to
consider and decide the matter. She went to Rev.
Mr. Allen for counsel, and laid the subject before
him. He soon saw that her mind was made up to
be a Christian, and that there was no occasion for
advising her in the matter. He simply advised her
to follow the convictions of her mind, and leave the
result with God. Her decision was soon made
known to the young gentleman, and the matrimonial
engagement dissolved. She soon united with the
church, and became a most exemplary, earnest
Christian. In about one year she was united in
marriage with Rev. H. B., a member of the Providence Conference. She entered upon her new
sphere of labor with a purpose to devote her time
and talents to the service of the Lord. Her prospects for usefulness were most encouraging; but
disease fastened itself upon her naturally delicate
constitution, and in a few months her spirit took its
upward flight to her heavenly home. Her death was
a Christian triumph.

In 1849 Rev. T. G. Carver, who had been ad-

mitted into the New England Conference on probation, was transferred to the Providence Conference,
and stationed at Chestnut Street, where he remained
two years. It was during this year that what is now
the Broadway Church was commenced on Federal
Street.

In 1851 and 1852 Rev. John Hobart was pastor
of this church.

CHURCH EDIFICE REMODELED.

During Mr. Hobart's pastorate the church edifice
was raised and remodeled, the steeple was finished,
the present organ introduced, and the church left
with an embarassing debt.

In 1853 and 1854 Rev. S. C. Brown was pastor.
The church prospered under the labors of Bro.
Brown.

In 1855 and 1856 Rev. Richard Livesey, now
gone to his rest, was pastor. Mr. Livesey is said to
have been an able and successful minister of the New
Testament.

In 1857 and 1858, Rev. George M. Carpenter.
The church this year shared in the gracious revival

7

which visited the whole country, and some interesting additions were made to the society.

In 1859 and 1860, Rev. J. A. M. Chapman. Bro. Chapman was a great favorite with the people of his charge, and on special occasions drew crowded congregations. The sub-bass of the organ got out of tune this year, creating no little discord in the society.

TRINITY CHURCH ORGANIZED.

It was in the year 1859 that a new interest was started, and a fifth church organized, known as the Trinity Church.

DEBT PAID ON CHESTNUT STREET CHURCH.

In 1861 and 1862 Rev. J. B. Gould was pastor. Bro. Gould was successful in removing a long standing debt, of more than $6,000, from the church property. Of the amount contributed, Hezekiah Anthony gave $2,800 and Dexter N. Knight $1,000. Bro. Gould taking a chaplaincy in the army during his second year, Rev. A. P. Aikin, a graduate from the Wesleyan University, took his place and labored with marked success until the close of the Conference year.

In 1863 and 1864, Rev. W. McDonald. The church and parsonage were repaired and newly painted. About the first of November, 1864, the pastor was stricken down by fever, which well nigh terminated his earthly being. For four months he lingered between life and death. But, by the constant and earnest prayers of the church and the blessing of God, he was restored. The pulpit was supplied the most of the time by Rev. H. V. Degen, of the New England Conference.

In 1865 and 1866 Rev. Mark Trafton was pastor. Mr. Trafton enjoyed uninterrupted prosperity during his two years. Some changes were made in the galleries of the church, and a large choir introduced, under the direction of Professors Tourjee and Snow, which added greatly to the attractions of the service. Perhaps the Chestnut St. Church has not been in a more prosperous state for many years, if ever, than at the close of Mr. Trafton's term of pastoral service. Mr. Trafton was succeeded by Rev. J. M. Bidwell, who is the present pastor.

EXHORTERS.

John F. Trescott.

SUNDAY SCHOOL SUPERINTENDENT.

Dutic Wilcox.

The present membership, including probationers, is 272.

HISTORY

OF

POWER STREET CHURCH.

In the latter part of the year 1832, a number of the most enterprising members of Chestnut Street Church, seeing the need of a Methodist Church on the east side of the city, and led on by such men as Daniel Field, Hezekiah Anthony, Joseph Fuller, Levi Webster, Job Andrews, James Lewis, Abner, David, and Capt. Abiza Hall, the enterprise was commenced and vigorously prosecuted. A subscription was made to purchase a lot, and begin the erection of a house of worship on the corner of South Main and Power Streets. The corner-stone of the new edifice was laid, with appropriate religious ceremonies, July 4, 1833. The house was dedicated Jan. 1, 1834, Rev. J. Horton preaching a very able sermon on the occasion, on the distinctive doctrines of Methodism.

Rev. C. K. True, having been admitted to the New England Conference on probation, and ap-

pointed to Bristol Circuit, as colleague of Rev. E.
K. Avery, until the Power Street Church should be
completed, now became colleague of Rev. J. Horton,
stationed at Chestnut Street, and on Jan. 5, the
Sabbath following the dedication, preached the first
Sabbath sermon in the new church from Isaiah 40 : 3,
" The voice of him that crieth in the wilderness, Pre-
pare ye the way of the Lord." The house was well
filled, and through the earnest labors of the youthful
evangelist many were added to the church. Mr.
True's health failing him through over-exertion, he
was obliged, reluctantly, to relinquish his charge
about the middle of the following March. Bro.
True speaks of his labors in Providence thus : " I
longed greatly in those days for the conversion of
sinners ; and, being a very early riser, I used to
walk the streets of Providence, long before the people were awake, praying for a revival of religion.
I had a delightful intimacy with my beloved colleague — Rev. Mr. Horton — and his family. That
meek-eyed, patient, intelligent wife, and those well
behaved children, I shall never forget. I little
thought then of the scenes which were before us in
the anti-slavery struggle, and that one of those boys

would fall a victim of liberty in the streets of New Orleans."

Mr. True leaving the charge, Rev. D. Patten, Jr., was appointed as his successor. Mr. Patten continued his labors until the session of Conference. During the labors of Messrs. True and Patten, about eighty members of Chestnut Street were transferred to the Power Street Church, and some forty were added by conversion, etc.

A Sabbath School was organized, numbering about one hundred scholars, and the society was, in every respect, in a most prosperous condition. God crowned their efforts with success.

April 1st, 1834, at a Quarterly Conference held in Power Street Church for both societies, it was resolved to divide the charge and call it Providence, East and West. From this time Power Street became an independent charge, and has so remained to this day.

It is said that Hezekiah Anthony, who took a deep interest in the establishment of this society, declared on the day of the dedication, that the church would never be successful; and gave as the reason, that they were ten minutes late in commencing the dedicatory services. If the remark was not a truthful prophecy, it was a most striking illustration of Mr. Anthony's promptness in business; for it is but just to say that a man of equal promptness in business is not often found in any community.

In 1834 Rev. H. H. White was the stationed preacher. He remained but one year, and was succeeded in 1835 and 1836 by Rev. A. U. Swinerton.

In 1837 Rev. Abel Stevens was appointed to this charge. His health failing, he was obliged to relinquish his charge at the end of the first year, and try a warmer climate. Mr. Stevens was a power in the pulpit, — so youthful, so earnest and eloquent; he attracted large crowds to hear him, and the society greatly regretted the necessity which compelled him to leave.

From November, 1838, to June, 1839, Rev. Richard Livesey supplied the pulpit with acceptance.

In 1839 and 1840 Rev. D. Fillmore was pastor. His labors were profitable to the society.

1841, Rev. C. S. Macreading. Mr. Macreading's labors were attended with a very remarkable revival. He remained but one year.

1842, Rev. E. M. Stickney.

1843, Rev. W. T. Harlow.

1844-5, Rev. A. U. Swinerton.

1846, Rev. E. B. Bradford.

1847–8, Rev. D. Wise.

During Mr. Wise's second year, some trouble arose with regard to the introduction of a musical instrument. The improvement was urged by a large number of influential members, and opposed by a still larger number, resulting in the withdrawal of some twenty members, who, uniting with others from Chestnut Street, organized the Mathewson Street Church.

A very gracious revival followed this secession, resulting in more than filling their depleted ranks.

1849–50, Rev. H. C. Atwater was the pastor. The revival commenced under Mr. Wise, continued through Mr. Atwater's entire administration, adding about ninety to the church.

1851–52, Rev. J. D. Butler. His ministry was successful. At first, as might have been expected after so extensive a revival as attended the labors of the two preceding pastors, there was, for a time, an apparent reaction. This continued for about six months, when the tide turned; and during the remainder of Mr. Butler's term there was a gradual revival, resulting in the conversion of ninety-nine souls. "My two years in Power Street," says Mr. Butler,

" I consider among the most successful in the course
of my labors in the church."

1853–54, Rev. J. Howson.

1855–56, Rev. J. Lovejoy.

1857–58, Rev. J. Mather.

1859–60, Rev. T. Ely.

Mr. Ely projected the plan of remodeling the
church, and securing the pews to the society. His
term of service closed before anything had been completed.

1861–62, Rev. II. Baylies was pastor.

POWER STREET CHURCH EDIFICE REMODELED.

Immediately on the appointment of Mr. Baylies to
this charge, measures were adopted for the alteration
and improvement of the church edifice. Rev. Mr.
Ely had the matter under advisement during his administration, and had met with more or less opposition ; but under Rev. Mr. Baylie the work was
prosecuted with vigor. The house was thoroughly
remodeled and made neat and attractive ; all the
pews being made over to the society so that they are
owned and rented by the society.

The house was re-opened for worship Jan. 29,

1862, the pastor preaching the sermon on the occasion.

1863–64, Rev J. B. Gould was pastor.

1865–66 Rev. G. M. Hamlin.

Bro. Hamlin's administration was a success. A goodly number were converted and added to the church and a debt on the church of $5,300 was provided for; so that this church reaches the Centenary year free from debt.

In 1867 Rev. J. Livesey was pastor.

Rev. J. M. Dean is the present pastor. The Power Street Church is in a hopeful state. Its location is not the most desirable for growth, but, under these disadvantages, its success has been commendable. It has not been without its troubles. Few churches in the Providence Conference have had a more stormy and checkered career.

But, through all these difficulties, a divine hand has guided it in its course, and preserved it from the destruction which has, again and again, seemed to threaten it.

Frederick P. Pearce,   Joseph Frankland,
Morris Deming,   Elisha J. Allen.

STEWARDS.

Philip H. Durfee,   Solomon Green,
Elery Millard,   Elisha J. Allen,
James Frankland,   Nath'l H. West,
Charles R. Leonard,   Joseph Frankland.
James Crawford,

CLASS LEADERS.

Joseph Frankland,   Elery Millard,
Wm. J. Spencer,   John B. Earle,
Geo. A. Taylor,   Frederick P. Pearce.

SUNDAY SCHOOL SUPERINTENDENT.

Solomon Green.

LOCAL PREACHER.

Samuel Griffin.

EXHORTER.

William T. Osmun.

The present membership of the church, including probationers, is 260.

HISTORY

OF

MATHEWSON STREET CHURCH.

During the year 1848 the Mathewson Street
Church was organized as the third Methodist church
in Providence. The difficulties in the Power Street
Church had determined a number of the members to
withdraw; among them Dr. Charles W. Fabyan.
Dr. Fabyan remarked to Rev. R. W. Allen, pastor
of the Chestnut Street Church, that he did not know
where to attend church. Bro. Allen replied, "It is a
good time to commence a new society, and you are
the man to lead off in it." Dr. Fabyan inquired,
"Where shall we meet for worship?" Bro. Allen
replied, "In one of the Halls." Arrangements were
soon made, and on Sunday, Oct. 1st, 1848, a congregation assembled for the first time in the old
Hoppin Hall, No. 33 Westminster Street, composed of members chiefly from Power Street and
Chestnut Street churches.

It was their opinion that the interests of the cause
of God, and of Methodism in the city, demanded
another Methodist Church ; and this first step was
an experiment by which to judge of the necessity of
the movement in the light of its results. To their
great joy, the first fruits gave promise of a rich har-
vest. The Hall was well filled, and Rev. Robert
Allyn, then in charge of the East Greenwich Semi-
nary, preached the first sermon from Psa. 20 : 5,
" In the name of our God we will set up our ban-
ners." The sermon, as well as the text, is said to
have been exceedingly appropriate, and contributed
much towards starting the new enterprise in the right
spirit. It revealed true piety as the sure and certain
ground of a church's life and prosperity. The following Sabbath, Oct. 8, Mr. Allyn preached again.
Oct. 15, Rev. Robert M. Hatfield preached. Oct.
22, Rev. David Patten, Jr., preached. From Oct.
29 to the next session of Conference, April, 1849,
Rev. W. Livesey was the pastor. The congregation
met for three Sabbaths without organization. On
Thursday evening, Oct. 19, they met for the purpose
of formal organization. Twenty-eight persons had
secured their letters, and became at this time the
original members of the Mathewson Street Metho-

dist Episcopal Church. The names of these members were as follows : Preston Bennett, Elizabeth S. Bennett, Charles C. Burnham, Elizabeth P. Burnham, Henry Baker, Susan Baker, Anna Briggs, Mary J. Bishop, Nicholas R. Easton, Maria Easton, Charles W. Fabyan, M. D., Pamelia C. Fabyan, Hannah Fraden, John Hoar, Mercy Hoar, Sarah A. Harris, Daniel Murry, Allen Monroe, Abby Monroe, Nathaniel N. Pratt, Abby F. Parker, Phila Sweetland, Elias Stoyles, Daniel Sisson, William A. Williams, Anna M. Williams, Josiah L. Webster, Helen M. Webster.

Twenty-one of the foregoing number were from Power Street, six from Chestnut Street, and one from East Greenwich.

FIRST OFFICIAL MEMBERS OF THIS CHURCH.

TRUSTEES.

David Sisson,	Preston Bennett,
Dr. C. W. Fabyan,	William B. Lawton,
Solomon Arnold,	William A. Williams,
Daniel Murry,	Nath'l R. Easton.

STEWARDS.

D. Sisson,	P. Bennett,

Dr. C. W. Fabyan,   C. W. Burnham,
N. R. Easton,   W. A. Williams.
H. Baker,   .

W. A. Williams,   D. Murry.
Josiah L. Webster,

Preston Bennett.

Seventeen of the original members have either re-moved from the city, joined other churches, or with-drawn; three only have died, and eight still remain members of the church (1867). Those who have died are, Phila Sweetland, William A. Williams and Anna Williams. Some of these names, though dead, yet speak.

The prosperity of this church during its early history is worthy of remark. From the first the hall was filled with earnest and devout worshipers. On the evening of the fourth Sabbath after the open-ing of the hall, the first opportunity was given for the seekers of religion to manifest their desires. Quite a large number responded to the invitation, asking the prayers of Christians. From that night onward, revival was the watchword of the church. Scarcely a week passed without more or less con-

versions, and there was not a communion service for
years, it is said, without accessions to the society.
At the end of the first six months their membership
had just doubled, having added 28 to their number.

In 1849 Rev. David Patten was appointed to this
charge, and his labors were greatly blessed to the
people. The hall was ever crowded with attentive
hearers, and many were the sheaves gathered for the
Master. At the end of Mr. Patten's first year there
were 112 in society.

The original members were permitted to welcome
to their communion, among these converts, most of
the children and youth of their own families; many
of whom are still active members of this or some
other branch of the church.

In 1850 Bro. Patten was returned, and continued to
preach in the hall. Some time in the month of June
of this year arrangements were made to erect a house
of worship. A site was selected on Mathewson
Street, and the members entered into the work with
their usual energy. The house was not completed
during Bro. Patten's pastorate. But to his exertions
the enterprise was greatly indebted.

In 1851 Rev. R. M. Hatfield was the pastor.
May 28th of this year the new church was dedicated

to the service of God. Rev. D. Patten preached the sermon on the occasion.

The society, now in possession of the best church edifice in the Conference, and with zeal greatly increased by such an opening field of usefulness, entered upon the work of leading men to God with new vigor and corresponding success. The house soon became too strait for them. Mr. Hatfield's energy and popularity drew crowds from all parts of the city. It is doubtful if the church was ever so crowded as during this year.

One rule adopted by the official members in the conduct of their prayer meetings is worthy of note. They agreed among themselves that in their meetings not one minute of time should run to waste. In adhering to this rule it was sometimes necessary for persons to speak twice; but this did not often occur. As the result of this rule their meetings were always interesting, and often seasons of remarkable power. The unconverted were necessarily attracted to their meetings, and large numbers were converted to God. The church reported at the end of the year 200 members and probationers. Mr. Hatfield remained with the church but one year, and was succeeded in 1852 by Rev. W. T. Harlow. Mr. Harlow continued his labors with this church two years, and they were years of more or less prosperity. About 25 members were added to the society the first year. During the second year there was a falling off in the membership. It was not expected that the immense congregation drawn by Mr. Hatfield would be retained.

In 1854 Rev. M. J. Talbot was appointed to the charge. He remained but one year. Slight additions were made to the membership this year.

In 1855 Rev. Henry S. White was, the pastor. He remained two years. Bro. White enjoyed the confidence of the people, and was blessed with large additions to the church. The first year the membership increased to about 275, and the second to about 300.

In 1857 Rev. F. Upham was the pastor. Few preachers have been more signally blessed in this church than Mr. Upham. He enjoyed an almost uninterrupted revival, which largely increased the membership of the society, leaving at the end of his second year about 350 in society.

In 1859 Rev. S. C. Brown was the pastor. He remained two years. The church was more or less affected by so large a number of the more active members of the church leaving, for the purpose of organizing the Trinity Church. The church felt the loss, and did not seem to rally readily from the shock. Other and prominent members leaving and uniting with other churches materially affected its prosperity. They were years of trial, both to the pastor and the church.

In 1861 Rev. S. Dean was appointed to the charge. Mr. Dean remained two years. He entered upon the work under some disadvantages, but these were soon removed, and by his superior pulpit abilities drew a large and appreciative congregation. Mr. Dean was successful. And it was generally conceded that no man had filled the pulpit of this church more ably, and generally more acceptably.

In 1863 Rev. J. H. McCarty was transferred from the New Hampshire to the Providence Conference, and stationed at this church. Mr. McCarty came highly recommended, and commenced his labors under very favorable auspices. Without the pulpit popularity of his predecessor, he still possessed qualities of head and heart which won for him the love and esteem of his people. His feeble health, and certain peculiarities of his church, rendered it difficult for him to accomplish all that was hoped might be done.

Mr. McCarty returned the second year. His labors during the second year were about as they were the first. There was more or less internal difficulty and personal disagreement in the society, which made it exceedingly unpleasant for the pastor and many of the members.

Mr. McCarty was returned the third year, but becoming somewhat dissatisfied with the state of things in the society, and finding his labors more or less unsuccessful, resigned his charge about the middle of the year, and was transferred to the Detroit Conference.

Rev. Seth Reed, stationed at Edgartown, Mass., was removed from his charge, for the purpose of taking the pastorate of this church made vacant by the withdrawal of Mr. McCarty.

In 1866 and 1867 Mr. Reed was re-appointed to the charge, and has labored with acceptance and profit. Its present pastor is Rev. Mark Trafton.

The Mathewson Street Church from its origin has sought to maintain the first position in the Providence Conference, and generally it has been successful. It has had, like other churches, its trials and internal disruptions; but for enterprise and success it has had few if any equals in the Providence Conference. May it find a symbol of its history in the "burning bush," though subjected to fiery trials, yet unconsumed. Its membership at present is 266.

The following is the officiary of the church:

LOCAL PREACHERS.

Wm. Gardiner,   Sidney Dean.

STEWARDS.

John Kendrick,   James Rothwell,
T. G. Eiswall,   E. Curtis,
P. M. Stone,   W. J. Mitchell,
P. B. Wright,   Moses Deming.
David Harris,

LEADERS.

Samuel Curry,   J. L. Webster,
John Crowell,   Samuel Boyd, Jr.,
A. J. Manchester,   Thomas Gardiner.
J. S. Latham,

SUNDAY SCHOOL SUPERINTENDENT.

Charles A. Webster.

HISTORY

OF

BROADWAY CHURCH.

In the year 1850 some of the members of Chestnut Street Church, feeling that a Sunday School was needed in the Northwest part of the city, took active measures to secure a place where such a school could be held. An old meeting-house, built and for a time occupied by Rev. John Tillinghast, and afterwards by the Calvinistic Baptists, situated on the corner of Dean and Federal Streets—now occupied for a dwelling house—was secured, and in the month of April of the same year a Sunday School was organized. Wm. K. Thurber was appointed superintendent. On the evening of the same Sabbath there was preaching in this house by Rev. T. G. Carver. Sabbath evening preaching was continued by the pastors of Chestnut, Power and Mathewson Streets. Under the labors of these pastors the work of God was more or less revived, until it seemed necessary to have a regular pastor.

Rev. Richard Donkersley, a superannuated member of the Providence Conference, was secured, and served the society for a time.

In the fall of the same year the services of Rev. C. Banning were secured, and regular Sabbath service was established. Bro. Banning's labors resulted in the conversion of quite a number of souls.

In 1851 Rev. D. Fillmore was appointed to the Federal Street Mission; but Rev. T. Ely, Presiding Elder, took the responsibility of allowing Bro. Banning to remain another year, greatly to the gratification of the people.

The first Board Meeting for the church was held April 28, 1851, at the house of W. K. Thurber.

The stewards were Harvey Dingley, Isaac Sperry, N. C. Briggs, and Edmond Kenyon. W. K. Thurber, Class Leader.

The year was one of unusual prosperity to the church. Bro. Banning's labors were greatly blessed among the people. He was greatly beloved by all, and general harmony prevailed.

In 1852, Rev. Moses Chase was appointed to the charge. He labored with his usual success for one year, and was succeeded in 1853 by Rev. J. Cady, who remained with the society three years,—the third

9

year supernumerary. The location of the church was unfavorable, and there was little hope of success without some change. At a Board Meeting held at the house of Bro. Cady, May 29, 1854, the feeling was general that something must be done or the enterprise must be abandoned. A committee, consisting of John Dean and William Barney, was appointed to see if the house formerly occupied by the Wesleyan Methodist Church, corner of Fountain and Franklin Streets, could not be secured. This church, which was organized in 1840, had failed to succeed, and their house was unoccupied.

At a Board Meeting, held at the house of Rev. J. Cady April 20, 1855, the committee before named reported that they had hired the Wesleyan Church for three hundred dollars per year, with the privilege of purchasing the same for three thousand dollars. It was voted to engage the house and immediately remove to it. It was voted at the same meeting to change the name of the society from Federal Street Mission to the Fourth Methodist Episcopal Church.

Sunday, April 22, the first service was held in this church. Sermon by the pastor, Rev. J. Cady.

July 25, 1855, a committee, consisting of Rev. J. Cady, preacher in charge, J. Dean, R. G. Cory and

Wilber Barney, were appointed to make arrangements for the purchase of the house of the Wesleyan Methodist Church. July 30th, the committee reported that they had made a satisfactory purchase of the church, and their report was accepted and the purchase sanctioned by the Board.

The first Board of Trustees were elected in August of this year. They were Rev. J. Cady, Robert G. Cory, John Dean, C. Mowry, R. W. Cady, T. Adderman, T. J. Gardiner, L. Arnold and W. Barney. In January, 1856, they secured their charter from the Legislature.

In 1856 Rev. W. Kellen was appointed to the charge, and remained one year.

In 1857 Rev. S. M. Carroll became the pastor, and remained two years. These years were not marked with remarkable prosperity. It was felt by all that even this location was not favorable, and that a more eligible site was imperatively demanded. As the Trinity Church enterprise was about being inaugurated, efforts were made to unite the two interests, but without success. For a time it was doubtful as to what would be the result.

In 1859 Rev. E. B. Bradford was appointed to the charge. After looking over the ground for a

time, it was judged expedient to make some change
in their church location at once. It was finally determined to purchase an eligible lot on Broadway
and remove their present church edifice on to it, and
sell their lot on Fountain Street. Through the inde-
fatigable labors of Mr. Bradford, this result was accomplished. The lot was purchased and the house
removed. A new front was added, and other important modifications made, so that the house presented all the appearance of a new church. It is due
to Mr. Bradford to say that his efforts were untiring.
He not only preached on the Sabbath, but performed
manual labor on the church from first to last. He
labored as few men could or would have done ; but
he had the satisfaction of seeing the top-stone brought
forth with rejoicing. The church, though left with
a few thousand dollars' debt, was in a better condition
than ever before. The pews were all owned by the
society, and rented for the benefit of the church. The
church as remodeled, was dedicated in September,
1860,—Rev. R. M. Hatfield preaching an edifying
sermon on the occasion.

In 1861 Rev. H. S. White became the pastor,
and remained nearly two years. He was successful,
and many additions were made to the society. Bro.

White; accepting a chaplaincy in the army, left a few months before the close of his second year and was succeeded in the charge by Rev. Alfred Wright, who served the church with acceptance during the remainder of the year.

In 1863 Rev. C. H. Paine was appointed to the charge. Bro. Paine labored with great acceptance. The congregation was greatly improved in numbers, the Sunday School largely increased, and all the interests of the church promoted. Bro. Paine remained with the church two years.

In 1865 Rev. J. B. Gould was pastor. Bro. Gould vacating the charge during his second year, the pulpit was supplied by Rev. S. Dean. This brings us to the Centenary year.

In 1867 Rev. V. A. Cooper became the pastor. It is but just to say that Broadway Church has labored under many embarrassments; and it was not until they had established themselves in their present location that they were in a condition to do much. Since their removal to Broadway they have prospered. The members have been devoted to the work, and have bravely and zealously labored to establish Methodism in that section of the city. May their labors be crowned with complete success.

The following are the official members :

TRUSTEES.

Thomas Adderman,	Wilber Barney,
Jacob F. Monro,	Christo. W. Mowry,
Perry G. Card,	Gilbert M. Steere,
H. S. Lamson,	Peleg H. Barnes.
Richard Lowe,	

STEWARDS.

Henry T. Salisbury,	Andrew J. Magoon,
Wm. L. Cook,	Horace S. Lamson,
Elisha J. Arnold,	John Robinson,
Gilbert M. Steere,	Peleg H. Barnes.
Thomas Adderman,	

CLASS LEADERS.

Richard Lowe,	W. N. Lansing.
Perry G. Card,	

SUNDAY SCHOOL SUPERINTENDENT.

Richard Lowe.

The present membership of the church, including probationers, is 202.

HISTORY

OF

SOUTH PROVIDENCE CHURCH.

The origin of the Methodist Church in South Providence was on this wise :—About the year 1854, at a missionary prayer meeting held in the Chestnut St. Church, Job Andrews and others made some remarks upon the importance of home missionary labor, in contrast with the foreign work. J. W. Bowdish challenged the brethren to unite with him in this work, and called attention to South Providence as a suitable and most promising field. The remarks called up an English brother by the name of Brown, who spoke of what he had already tried to do in establishing a Sunday School in South Providence ; but from a variety of causes, principally want of aid, he had nearly abandoned the enterprise. He seconded most heartily the measure, and was himself ready to engage in the work.

Mr. Bowdish, believing this to be a providential opening, determined at once to engage in the work

He endeavored to enlist Mr. Andrews in the enterprise, believing that a man of his talent and influence would be of great service; but for some reason he declined.

Soon after this meeting a Sunday School was organized in Mitchell's Hall, formerly occupied by the Spiritualists. At first the school was small, but continued to increase in numbers until it became necessary to secure a larger place. Lyceum Hall on Eddy Street was obtained, where the school had ample room.

In 1856 South Providence appears on the Minutes for the first time as a Mission, Rev. Jonathan Cady preacher in charge. November 30th of this year the first Quarterly Conference was held, Rev. C. H. Titus presiding elder. The official members of the church at this time were:

CLASS LEADER.

R. Brown.

STEWARDS.

Albert Cutter,   Samuel Hancy,   S. C. Read.

The report of the Sunday School showed, 1 school, 12 officers and teachers, 100 scholars, 266 vols. in library, 20 in infant class.

In 1857 Mr. Cady was returned to the Mission. At the last Quarterly Conference for this year, held Jan. 24, 1858, there were reported 20 members in society. Sunday School—Officers and teachers, 10; scholars, 100; in infant class, 20; vols. in library, 400.

In 1858 the Mission was left to be supplied. John F. Trescott, a member of Chestnut Street Church, was invited to take charge of the work until a preacher could be obtained. Mr. Trescott received an Exhorter's license at the first Quarterly Conference of this year. At the second Quarterly Conference held at Chestnut Street, his license was revoked, on account, we believe, of some peculiar theological views which he held and publicly advocated. He continued, notwithstanding, to labor with acceptance and profit in the Sunday School and social meetings. The desk was supplied during the year by different Local Preachers.

At a Quarterly Conference held Jan. 23, 1859, Rev. J. E. Risley was appointed to the charge, in connection with Bro. Trescott. But for some reason Bro. Risley's stay was brief. "After the division of the receipts of a Fair and Festival," says Bro. Trescott, "between Bro. Risley and myself, which amounted to $15 each, Bro. Risley retired from the field and I had the pleasure of turning my $15 over to the society for church purposes, which was the first contribution for the purchase of a lot for a church. What has become of it I do not know."

In 1860 Rev. Charles M. Winchester, a member of Broadway M. E. Church, came to labor with this church as preacher and Sunday School superintendent. The society was at this time very feeble, and every part of the work languished. There were a few brethren who loved and trusted the Lord, and were determined to maintain the Methodist form of worship in South Providence. Among them may be named D. J. Burgess, J. A. Thornton, A. W. Potter, Z. Petterson, A. Newberg and J. Pierce. By the united effort of pastor and people a measure of prosperity was enjoyed by the society.

In October, 1863, Mr. Winchester, believing it to be his duty to enter the service of his country, resigned his charge and assisted in recruiting a company for the 12th Reg't R. I. V., and enlisted himself in Company B. He served in the regiment until its discharge in July, 1863.

In the absence of Mr. Winchester the charge was supplied chiefly by J. W. Bowdish.

On the return of Mr. Winchester from the war,
he took charge of the church again. Matters pro-
gressed as prosperously as could well be expected
under the circumstances, until, without any notice,
their hall was sold to the town of Cranston for school
purposes, and the society was left, unexpectedly, without a place of worship. In this their time of need,
the brethren of the Baptist Church extended to them
a cordial invitation to worship with them, and to use
their church for the Sunday School, until such time
as they should have a place of their own. The offer
was accepted.

About the 1st of January, 1866, the Sons of
Temperance completed their large hall, which was
immediately hired by the society at an annual rent of
$350. This at once gave them ample accommoda-
tions, and several were added to the society.

Near the close of 1867 Mr. Winchester yielded
to an urgent invitation to become Chaplain of the
Seaman's Bethel, Providence, and for the purpose of
doing so resigned his charge.

It is but just to say, that during the long period
which Mr. Winchester served this church unbroken
harmony and the best of feeling existed, and bonds
of Christian friendship were formed which will con-

tinue during life and will doubtless be renewed in eternity.

In 1868 Rev. S. T. Benton was appointed to this charge. By the aid of the "Domestic Missionary and Sunday School Society," organized by the several Methodist churches in Providence, the South Providence Church bids fair to become a self-sustaining as well as vigorous society.

This church has always been feeble, and consequently has labored under great embarrassments. It has done well with the means at its disposal. May it long survive, with increasing prosperity; and as a city on a hill may its light be seen by many a wanderer from God, who shall rejoice in the light, having by it been led to the Saviour of sinners.

HISTORY

OF

TRINITY M. E. CHURCH.

At a meeting of the Official Board of Mathewson Street Church, Dec. 17, 1858, Dr. G. S. Stevens proposed the establishment of a Methodist Mission in Lester Hall, Cranston Street. After a careful consideration of the subject it was voted that unless at least eight hundred dollars could be secured to meet the expenses for one year, they could not approve the enterprise. A committee consisting of J. L. Webster, John Kendrick and Dr. G. S. Stevens were appointed to solicit subscriptions and report the result to the Board. At the next Board meeting, Dec. 27, the committee reported that after securing subscriptions to the amount of four hundred dollars, they had ceased their efforts, for the reason that several members of the Board were opposed to the enterprise. The committee was therefore discharged at their own request. Two weeks later, Dr. G. S. Stevens hired Lester Hall for three months for Sundays, and for Wednesday evenings, for religious services, and engaged Rev. Andrew McKeown to supply the pulpit. The first service—a prayer meeting —was held in one of the ante-rooms of the hall, Jan. 16th, 1859, at 9 1-2 o'clock, A. M. The following persons were present: Dr. G. S. Stevens, John Kendrick, W. J. Martin, W. F. Lawton, Sam'l Robinson, A. F. Hopkins, C. W. Thurber, J. H. Merideth, Geo. H. Chenery, Thos. Seckell, Thos. Barker, A. Southwick and Rev. A. McKeown, who took charge of the services. The meeting is said to have been one of unusual interest. Bro. McKeown preached three sermons the same day in this hall, to congregations varying from one to three hundred. Dr. Stevens is said to have laid it down as a rule at this prayer meeting, that old-fashioned Methodist responses, such as "amen," etc., would always be in order at any time during the exercises of the day and evening. Collections were taken at each service, amounting to thirteen dollars.

At the next Quarterly Conference of the Mathewson Street Church, the preacher in charge, Rev. F. Upham, brought up the subject of this new Mission, and the following resolution was, after some discussion, passed.

RESOLVED. That we legalize the enterprise recently started in Lester Hall, by certain members of the Mathewson Street Church, and hereby sanction the same.

A notice was given Jan. 30th, that on the following Sabbath a Sunday School would be organized to take the place of the forenoon service. At the Board meeting of the Mathewson Street Church on the following evening, some objection having been made to the organization of the school as irregular, and without authority, after discussion it was voted to commence the school, and the following officers were appointed: Dr. G. S. Stevens, Superintendent; Wm. J. Martin, Secretary; Charles A. Williams, Librarian. John Kendrick was chosen Treasurer of the Mission. It was also voted to lend the Mission School books from the Mathewson St. Library.

February 6th, 1859, Rev. A. McKeown opened the services with reading the Scriptures, singing and prayer; after which he stated the action of the Mathewson Street Board, and announced the officers of the school. The officers proceeded at once to organize the school into classes. Fourteen classes of children under fifteen years of age were formed. Two Bible Classes were formed; one under the charge of Rev. A. McKeown, and the other under the charge of Nathan B. Hall. There were present one hundred and thirty-four, of whom, fifty-two adults and fifty-seven children became members of the school. The school increased rapidly. On the following Sunday there were 160 present; the third Sunday 181; and the fourth 257.

It had been arranged that Bro. McKeown, or some other preacher from the Conference, should be sent to take charge of this Mission. But at the session of the Providence Conference, held in Fall River, March 30th, 1859, a communication was received by the Presiding Elder, Rev. C. H. Titus, from the members of the official Board of Mathewson St. Church, to the effect that they thought it not desirable that a minister should be appointed to the Mission, as it had not secured a sufficient number of men of character and influence to warrant the attempt to form a new church organization. But at a meeting of the friends of the Mission, held the same evening, March 30th, it was resolved to ask the Presiding Elder to organize them as the Trinity M. E. Church, and supply them with a preacher. The following petition was drawn up and signed:

"PROVIDENCE, March 30, 1859.

To the Presiding Elder of the Providence District of the Providence Conference :—

We the undersigned, members of the Mathewson St. M. E. Church in this city, and of other churches, desirous of forming a new church organization to be known as the Trinity M. E. Church in Providence, hereby respectfully request the Providence Annual Conference to send us a preacher, who may so organize us and serve us for the ensuing year. We have raised by subscription one thousand dollars towards defraying the expenses for one year.

We would also respectfully represent that we have a convenient place of worship, a good congregation, and an organized Sunday School of 250 members.

(Signed) Thomas H. Barker, Mary A. Barker, Geo. H. Chenery, Marcy B. Gould, Arnold F. Hopkins, Charles F. Hull, Caroline B. Hull, Wm. F. Lawton, Martha B. Lawton, Thomas J. Monroe, Louisa Monroe, William J. Martin, Harriet A. Macreading, Samuel Robinson, Andrew S. Southwick, Dr. G. S. Stevens, Hannah W. Stevens, Isabella Timpson, Sarah W. Walker, Edna A. Lee, Betsey Persons, Catherine Benson."

Wm. F. Lawton and G. S. Stevens were appointed a committee to represent the Mission at the Conference.

In consequence of these conflicting representations no preacher was appointed to the Mission by the presiding Bishop—Ames—but the whole matter was referred to the presiding elder of the district, Rev. G. M. Carpenter, with authority to organize the church and supply the pulpit.

It was soon evident that a minister at Lester Hall was a necessity. Accordingly the next week, Rev. Wm. McDonald, greatly against his wishes, was transferred from the New England Conference and stationed at Trinity Church, or what was to be ; or, as one of our Church papers had it—" transferred to Providence and stationed on the Common, to dig or die."

It would transcend the limits assigned to these pages to detail all the seeming Providential circumstances connected with this arrangement. It is enough to say that the preacher came, and on the 24th of April, 1859, commenced his labors. The first sermon preached was from Acts 10 : 29. The church was organized the same day, consisting of 34 members and 1 probationer. The following were the original members :

Thos. H. Barker,　　　　Mrs. Mary A. Barker,
Miss Mary A. Barker,　　Geo. H. Chenery,
Laura M. Davis,　　　　Thomas J. Gardiner,
Sarah J. Griffin,　　　　Nancy B. Gould,
Frances B. Gardner,　　Amelia J. Gardner,
James G. Green,　　　　Hannah Green,
Hary E. Green,　　　　Arnold F. Hopkins,
Charles F. Hull,　　　　Caroline B. Hull,
Wm. F. Lawton,　　　　Martha B. Lawton,
Wm. H. Leavett,　　　　Wm. J. Martin,
Thos. J. Monroe,　　　　Louisa Munroe,
Harriet A. Macreading,　Elizabeth Persons,
Samuel Robinson,　　　G. S. Stevens,
Hannah W. Stevens,　　Mary Slocum,
Orlando Smith,　　　　Andrew S. Southwick,
Isabella Timpson,　　　Joseph B. White,
Mary D. Wickson,　　　Sarah M. Walker.

Robert Timpson was received on probation the same day.

The first Quarterly Conference was held at the house of Dr. G. S. Stevens, May 5th, 1859. There were present Rev. G. M. Carpenter, Presiding Elder, Rev. Wm. McDonald, preacher in charge, Dr. G. S. Stevens and W. J. Martin, Leaders ; and Thos. J. Gardiner, Wm. F. Lawton, Chas. F. Hull, Jas.

G. Green and Samuel Robinson, who were appointed
Stewards.

OFFICIAL MEMBERS FOR THE FIRST YEAR.

TRUSTEES.

Dr. G. S. Stevens,	T. J. Gardiner,
C. F. Hull,	S. A. Edmond.

W. F. Lawton ; appointed Dec. 2d, 1859.

STEWARDS.

T. J. Gardiner,	W. F. Lawton,
C. F. Hull,	J. G. Green,

S. Robinson ; appointed May 5th, 1859.

T. H. Eston, app. at 2d Quarterly Conference.

LEADERS.

Dr. G. S. Stevens,	W. J. Martin.
Afterwards,	T. H. Eston,
S. A. Edmond,	W. F. Lawton.

SUNDAY SCHOOL SUPERINTENDENT.

Dr. G. S. Stevens.

The church was now fully organized, and in run-
ning order. The hall, which would accommodate
some five hundred persons, was filled each Sabbath.
The social meetings were seasons of special interest,
as all seemed hopeful and willing to contribute their

all to the enterprise. The conversion of souls was almost as frequent as Sabbaths, and the Sunday School soon became, in every respect, a model school, and "Christian Hill," as it was called in derision, felt the moral influence of this new element of power in their midst. We were informed by the Police that it did not require more than half the force to maintain order in that section of the city, as it did before this church was organized. We could give accounts of many of the most abandoned characters who were reclaimed.

Our hall being too small to accommodate the people who desired to attend, it was thought best to make an effort to build a more commodious house of worship. Consequently on the 15th of July, 1859, Dr. G. S. Stevens and Thomas J. Gardiner were appointed a building committee by the Quarterly Conference, to build or procure a house of worship. Wm. F. Lawton was afterwards added to the committee. Many locations were examined and estimates made, without any favorable results.

It here becomes our duty to record faithfully one of the most unpleasant chapters in the history of this church ; a matter out of which has grown many false representations, made through either design, ignorance or forgetfulness, and we could hope for the sake of Christianity that it were the latter.

Mr. Perry Davis, known in all parts of the world as the "Pain Killer" man, had, by the extensive sale of his "Pain Killer" amassed considerable wealth. But his liberality was beyond his income. Providence, in our judgment, has never been blessed with a man of more generous impulses. He was a liberal Baptist, discarding many of the cardinal tenets of the denomination. He had erected a substantial brick church on Stewart Street, at an expense of some $36,000, in which a Baptist Church had worshiped a number of years, Mr. Davis paying a large portion of the expenses. He had urged the church to take some steps to pay for the house, or at least a part of what it had cost him. But thinking that Mr. Davis would finally give them the property, no effort was attempted. Mr. Davis at last offered them the whole property for the sum of $12,000, giving them to understand that if this offer was not accepted he should dispose of the house. A subscription was started, and after a few thousands had been subscribed was abandoned.

Mr. Davis becoming exceedingly dissatisfied with the course taken, resolved to sell the house if he could find proper parties to buy. Stating his grievances one day to Mr. Geo. M. Butts, a well known broker of Providence, through whom Mr. Davis often negotiated loans, Mr. Butts remarked that if he desired to sell his church he thought he could find him a purchaser. He said he would sell the property for $16,000, four thousand more than he had offered it to his own church. Mr. Butts communicated the fact to Dr. Stevens, and he to some of the leading members of the Trinity Church. Mr. Butts was informed that the Trinity Church would purchase Mr. Davis' Church for the sum named. The bargain was completed about the 20th of October.

The concurrent testimony of Geo. M. Butts, Esq., Dr. G. S. Stevens, Thos. J. Gardiner, and the pastor of the church, shows that up to this time no word had been uttered with regard to a " Free Church " as a condition of purchase, out of which, ostensibly, all the trouble arose. There had been talk of a free church, if it could be established; but no word had been uttered to the effect that the church should be free, or abandoned, or that Mr. Davis was to own one half of the church, etc. As Mr. Davis was old and infirm, the members of Trinity Church thought it advisable to have some memorandum of the contract with him; consequently, Thomas J. Gardiner secured a properly drawn document, and in company with Dr. Stevens called on Mr. Davis, October 28th, in the evening, and stated to him the action of the church and what they had done. Mr. Davis expressed a perfect willingness to give a bond for the property. The document was handed to Mr. Davis, who looked it over and then requested Mr. Gardiner to read it, which he did twice, Mr. Davis suggesting some change in the time fixed for giving possession, which was done, and Mr. Davis signed the bond.

About the middle of November it was reported that Mr. Davis had concluded not to let the Trinity Church have the house. In the mean time every effort was made that could be made to induce Mr. Davis to cancel his obligation to the Trinity Church. Committees were appointed, and grave Doctors of Divinity attempted to alarm Mr. Davis by telling him that a refusal to allow the Baptists to retain the house would seriously affect the sale of his " Pain Killer," etc. On the evening of Nov. 23d, the pastor, in connection with Dr. G. S. Stevens and Thos. J. Gardiner, called on Mr. Davis to ask an explanation of the reports. He informed us frankly that under no arrangement would he give us a deed of the church—that with him the bargain was up, and that he should not give us a deed until he was obliged to. The only reason which he assigned for not fulfilling his obligation, was what he claimed to be an obligation on the part of Trinity Church to make it a Free Church, an obligation never given directly or indirectly, and never existed except in the imagination of Mr. Davis. He himself acknowledged that it was not in the contract, but it was in his mind.

It is true that the members of Trinity Church did talk of, and intended to make the church free, but the idea never originated with Mr. Davis, and was no part of the conditions of sale. It was soon found that Mr. Davis had sold his church to a Mr. John W. Smith, a member of the Stewart Street Church, and a clerk in Mr. Davis' employ, and a man known to be worth no such money as was professedly paid for the church. The whole transaction was an effort to prevent the Trinity Church from securing their just claim. In view of Mr. Davis' utter refusal to fulfill his obligation, there was no other course left to the Trinity church but to resort to legal measures. This was reluctantly done. The case was brought before the court, and decided in favor of Trinity Church. Appeal was taken, and the case was carried from one

11

term of court to another until the fall of 1863. Mr.
Davis dying in the mean time, left the matter in the
hands of his heirs. Such had been the feeling in the
Baptist Churches of the State, and such the long
controversy, that the Trinity Church had lost much
of their former interest in the matter, and judged it
would be for the best to accept of a proposition made
by Mr. Davis' heirs to pay them $1650, and relin-
quish their claim on the church. On the 3d of
March, 1864, the long-standing dispute was settled
upon these terms.

It is but just to say that the members of Trinity
Church never regarded Mr. Davis as responsible as
some other parties for this refusal to fulfill his written
obligation. They have always believed that had
he been left to act without such influences being
brought to bear upon him as would doubtless have
induced other men, with less of the infirmities of age
and of a more retentive memory, to have yielded, he
would have done differently. Mr. Davis had given
too many proofs of being a sincere, honest Christian
man, to allow us to believe that he would have been
guilty of a cool, deliberate, intelligent purpose to do
what all honest men would pronounce a most palpa-
ble wrong. Mr. Davis was little more than a machine

operated by other parties, who seemed determined to carry their points without reference to justice or moral obligation.

If we have judged men and motives incorrectly, or if others have acted without reference to justice, believing that the end would justify the means, may a merciful God forgive us for false judging on the one hand, and from unjust action on the other.

The success which attended the efforts of the members of Trinity for the first two years was all that could have been anticipated. The membership at the close of the second year was 185 ; an increase of 150 in two years.

In 1861 Rev. W. F. Farrington was transferred from the Maine to the Providence Conference, and became pastor of this church. He remained two years. The society continued to prosper, and numbered at the close of Mr. Farrington's term, in full and on trial, 225.

In 1863 Rev. James D. Butler became the pastor, and remained three years. Bro. Butler was cordially received by the society, and entered upon his work with his usual diligence and energy.

In the fall of 1863 the society began to consider how they should bring their unhappy church contro-

versy with Mr. Davis to an end. It was proposed
to make it a subject of prayer. At a Board meeting
held in January, 1864, a committee was appointed
to wait upon the heirs of Mr. Davis and propose a
settlement; and on the 3d of March following the
matter was arranged and settled between the two
churches, as formerly stated.

Mr. Butler reported at the close of his first year,
members and probationers, 210. With this falling
off in the membership from the last year, there were
still forty-eight converted under his labors. The
general impression prevailed that a new church should
be erected on Cranstan Street. But it was proposed
to make it a subject of prayer; "and we think," says
Rev. Mr. Butler, "that in answer to prayer we were
directed to the best location in the city of Providence,"
which is the one the church now occupies.

Excavations were commenced for laying the foun-
dation of the new church, March 26th, 1864. The
corner stone was laid June 24th, 1864, with impos-
ing Masonic ceremonies. Prayer by the Rev. W.
McDonald, and an address by Rev. S. Dean. The
church was commenced with the understanding that
it should be free, and should cost about $12,000.
But in consequence of the rise in the price of mate-

rial and labor, it was soon found that it would cost much more than at first contemplated. In the fall of 1864 the Trustees commenced holding Trustee prayer meetings. They met at Dr. Stevens', and after hearing from him that, financially, they were in a bad condition, it was proposed that before entering upon business they should each offer prayer. They accordingly knelt and began to cry to God; "and such manifestations of divine power," says Rev. Mr. Butler, who was present, "were scarcely ever witnessed before. Very soon after this we obtained some heavy subscriptions. So we continued to pray and work."

The house was completed and dedicated May 31st, 1865. Sermon by Rev. M. L. Scudder, D. D.

Mr. Butler remarks at this point, that "from the very beginning until now, the enterprise has been carried on by prayer and faith." And while they adhered to that policy God aided them, but when that course was abandoned, progress was at an end.

It becomes necessary here to record another unhappy chapter in the history of this church. Dr. G. S. Stevens, who had been the prime mover in this enterprise from the first, and who had done more than any other man to promote its interests, became, about this time, disaffected. It is due the doctor to say, that had it not been for his indomitable perseverance and almost superhuman efforts, the church would never have been built, nor would the society have had an existence at all; and his subsequent course was a cause of great sorrow to his friends.

It was sometime during the month of September of this year, that Dr. Stevens commenced reading the proof-sheets of a book entitled "The Constitution of Man," by Dr. Hatch. It was evident to his friends that the reading of this book had a powerful effect upon his mind, as well as his views and feelings in regard to Trinity Church. He was soon heard to say that he had lost all interest in the church, and did not care whether the house was paid for or not. He remarked one day to the pastor, Rev. Mr. Butler, that the house would have to be sold and go into other hands. Mr. Butler says: "I went home and laid the subject before the Lord, and obtained an answer which I delivered to the doctor the next day. I said, 'Doctor, that house will not go out of our hands. The Lord gave us that location in answer to prayer. He gave it to Trinity Church, and it will never go out of their hands.' The doctor replied,

'The church will be sold, and I shall go with it.'"
The sequel shows who was the true prophet.

That the doctor had the best interests of Trinity
Church at heart, there can be no doubt; and that he
labored to build up that church and Sunday School,
as few men have labored, there is the clearest evidence. That he became infatuated by certain persons, and that through those influences came very near
swamping the church, there is no question. While
great credit is due Dr. Stevens for his almost unpar-
alleled efforts in establishing Trinity Church, and securing the erection of their present house of worship,
it is to be regretted that he should have finally taken
the course he did.

Providentially, about this time, Dexter N. Knight,
a member of Chestnut St. Church, was induced to
leave and unite with Trinity. He was a God-send
to the society, for it is the belief of the writer, that
had not this event occurred the church edifice must
have been sold and the society scattered. Mr. Knight
took charge of the Sunday School, at this time numbering more than 400 members, and which under
the superintendency of Dr. Stevens had become the
model school of Providence, and carried it forward
with remarkable ability and success.

Here closes Mr. Butler's three years with this
church. They had been years of trial and triumph
to both pastor and people. But no man was more
honored and beloved by his people than was Mr.
Butler. He left the society in a very delightful religious state, with a revival in progress. There were in
society 184 members, and 46 probationers.

In 1866 Rev. D. H. Ela was appointed to Trinity
Church, and commenced his labors Sunday, April
1st. Such was the financial embarrassment of the
church that a committee was appointed by the Providence Conference on the subject, who reported in
favor of appropriating one half the Conference collections for the Church Extension Society, to the
amount of $7,000, for its relief. It was soon found
that the church was in debt more than $28,000.
There were bills against the Sunday School amounting to about $800; the whole, with the interest
thereon, amounting to more than $30,000. The so-
ciety had paid, up to this time, to the utmost of their
ability, nearly all the members being poor.

The Methodist churches of Providence, seeing the
perilous condition of Trinity, rallied to save it. A
meeting of the friends of the enterprise was called at
Chestnut St. Church, April 8th. All the churches

gave up their meetings in favor of this. Rev. M. Trafton presided. A statement of the condition of Trinity was made ; after which several ministers and laymen addressed the meeting, and subscriptions to the amount of $17,000 were made. This was a good beginning. Subscriptions were subsequently procured by D. N. Knight, and the pastor, Rev. D. H. Ela. But little more was done until the summer of 1867, when strenuous efforts were made to complete the work. In December of this year the pastor laid the case before a meeting of the official boards of the several churches in the city. By the favorable and generous action of the meeting, arrangements were made by which the entire amount was provided for.

Of these subscriptions D. N. Knight contributed $5,100, Hezekiah Anthony 1,500, Jeremiah Knight 1,000, John Kendrick 650, James Davis 600, W. S. Huntoon 550, A. and W. Sprague 500, Trinity Sunday School 1,500, Mathewson Street Sunday School 375, etc. And thus the work was completed " because the people had a mind to work." Taking it all in all, this is one of the most remarkable church enterprises ever undertaken in New England.

Notwithstanding these financial embarrassments, the spiritual interests of the church were not suffered to languish. The revival which commenced under Bro. Butler continued with remarkable power. At the close of Mr. Ela's first year there were 238 members and 50 probationers; and at the close of his second year there were 250 members and 38 probationers. The Sunday School numbers 560 members, with an average attendance of more than 400. It has been pre-eminently a revival school through its whole history. It has been the scene of some of the most blessed manifestations of the power of God.

Here we must conclude our somewhat extended history of Trinity Church. It had a providential origin, as it has had a remarkable history. It has been one of the most earnest, laborious and successful churches ever established in the city of Providence. May it long continue to proclaim a free salvation, and gather in from the lanes and highways of the city the neglected and the unsaved; and in eternity may it be known that many were born for glory here.

The present officers of the church:

LEADERS.

A. R. Lilley,	T. H. Esten,
O. H. Fernald,	W. F. Cady,
A. D. Litchfield,	J. Gaddis.

The present membership of the church, including probationers, is 281.

HISTORY

OF

ASBURY M. E. CHURCH.

The Asbury M. E. Church, located in the northern part of the city of Providence,—called in the Minutes of the Providence Conference for 1868, Asbury Mission,—is the youngest branch of the Methodist Church in this city. Its origin was on this wise: After a careful, earnest and prolonged discussion by the Union Board,—composed of official members of the several Methodist churches in the city,—of various plans for Church Extension, a committee of three was appointed, viz : Rev. J. Livesey, T. J. Gardiner and J. Burton, to ascertain if any convenient room or hall could be procured in the northern part of the city for the purpose of holding a Sunday School and other religious services. After diligent inquiry, the committee reported that the Mooshausic Engine Room, on Mill Street was unoccupied and could be procured.

Application was made to the municipal authorities, and permission was obtained to occupy the room for the purposes desired.

Friday evening, March 13, 1868, at a meeting of
the members and friends of Methodism residing in
that section of the city, held in the Engine Room, it
was resolved to proceed immediately to gather and
organize a Sunday School ; and further, to establish
such other religious services as they might be able to
maintain. Sunday, March 22d, at 9 A. M., a
few devoted and earnest Christians gathered at the
place to invoke the divine blessing upon the new enterprise. At 10 1-2 A. M., 76 adults and children
were enrolled and arranged into classes, under the su-
perintency of J. C. Jacobs, of the Broadway M. E.
Church. At 3 P. M., a congregation of about 130
assembled to listen to the opening sermon, preached
by Rev. J. Livesey, of the Power St. Church. At
7 P. M. an excellent prayer meeting was held. The
divine presence was powerfully manifested, and heaven
seemed to smile approvingly upon this new effort for
the extension of the Redeemer's kingdom. So encouraging had been the indications in all these services, that it was decided to apply at once to the
Providence Conference, to assemble that week, for the
appointment of a pastor to the charge. Rev. J.
Livesey was appointed, and entered at once upon his
labors.

Sunday, April 5, 1868, the Asbury M. E. Church
was organized, consisting of 26 members and 7 probationers—total, 33. During the first three months
the membership nearly doubled; and there is every
prospect that the church will soon become self-sustaining and one of the most prosperous in the city.
They have as yet no house of worship, but active
steps are being taken for the immediate erection of a
chapel, which shall accommodate the church and Sunday School; and it is confidently expected that very
soon they will sit "beneath their own vine and fig-
tree," to worship Him who has thus far so signally
prospered their enterprise.

The officers of the church and society are as follows :

TRUSTEES, ELECTED APRIL 21, 1868.

Morris Deming,　　　George W. Cady,
Philip B. Stiness,　　Jason A. Bidwell.
John Burton,

STEWARDS, ELECTED APRIL 21, 1868.

Morris Deming,　　　James C. Jacobs.
John Burton,　　　　W. H. White,
W. T. Morehead,　　John W. Foster.

CLASS LEADERS, ELECTED APRIL 21, 1868.

John W. Foster,   Morris Deming,
James C. Jacobs,   David Taylor.

OFFICERS OF THE SUNDAY SCHOOL.

J. C. Jacobs,   Superintendent.
J. Burton,   Assistant Sup.
P. B. Stiness, Jr.,   Sec'ry and Treasurer.
C. K. Melville,   Librarian.
—— D'Wolff,   Assistant Lib.

Vols. in Library, 400.

CONCLUSION.

We have faithfully traced the history of Methodism in Providence, from its introduction by the devoted, the indomitable Freeborn Garrettson, in 1787, to the eighty-first year of its existence. We have noted its mustard-seed-like origin and feeble growth; — the multiplied difficulties it has had to encounter from the poverty of its friends and the opposition of its enemies; and yet we have seen it outlive and outgrow all these discouragements, until the little one has become a thousand, and the handful of corn in the earth in the top of the mountain is beginning to shake like Lebanon ; and Methodism, once dishonored, reviled and scouted, emerging from "alley" and "kitchen," to occupy a respectable, yea, honorable position among the long standing churches of the city of Roger Williams. May its members never forget the hole of the pit whence they were digged, but ever learn to give all glory to Him who has made them all they are ; and may past successes stimulate to renewed efforts to "spread scriptural holiness," until the "kingdoms of this world shall become the kingdom of our Lord and of his Christ. Then shall one like unto the Son of Man be ever found walking in the midst of these "seven golden candlesticks" to make them lights of supernatural brilliancy, and protect them from the handof him who would extinguish their burning.